Praise for *Orname*

T0009694

Finalist for the 2021 PEN Translation Prize
The Guardian, "Top 10 Books about Colombia"
Southwest Review, "10 Must-Read Books of 2020"

"With pitch-black comedy, *Ornamental,* nimbly translated by Lizzie Davis, channels the ways that egomaniacs in science and art—in any field—rise to the top, up the pyramid of capitalism. . . . The rhythm of Cárdenas's writing compels and reassures, as if driven by the very humanity the lab has helped suppress."
 —Nathan Scott McNamara, *The New York Times*

"A work of subtlety and restraint. . . . What makes *Ornamental* so deeply affecting, however, is not that its pages come together to form a beautiful work of exterior art—though [they do]—but its ability to cast unease on our interior worlds. . . . Brilliantly executed and cleverly translated, *Ornamental* leaves us with a fresh understanding of the creation of art and the nature of meaning-making." **—Dashiel Carrera,** *Los Angeles Review of Books*

"In his thrilling novel *Ornamental,* Colombian art critic, translator, curator, and renowned author Juan Cárdenas masterfully tells the tale of the junction of an experimenting doctor, his wife, and his subsidized voluntary narcotic patient. . . . Expertly translated by seasoned editor Lizzie Davis."
 —Ellie Simon, *World Literature Today*

"In spare and economical prose, Cárdenas sketches a highly stratified world, where drugs link high society and neighborhoods that are 'a single crush of old houses and ruins.' . . . The overall effect offers both thrills and chills." **—*Publishers Weekly***

"[An] absurdist critique of class inequality. . . . Cárdenas also dabbles in art criticism and curation and uses that knowledge to acidic effect in a social drama that borders on the phantasmagorical. . . . With captivating moments." *—Kirkus*

"This is the first of Cárdenas's novels to be translated into English, with hopefully more to come, as he's a supremely talented and original writer. *Ornamental* is a strange, dystopian tale about medical trials, in which a doctor studies women addicted to a mysterious recreational drug. Drugs will sadly always be associated with Colombia, but Cárdenas's surreal examination of addiction and compulsion is a unique and necessary contribution to the conversation." **—Julianne Pachico, *The Guardian***

"An exhilarating, slippery narrative where the reader knows much truth can be found, if only they can figure out how to decipher it. . . . Cárdenas's prose is economical yet lyrical; many of his images are veritable objets d'art. . . . Lizzie Davis has done a spectacular job rendering Cárdenas's novel in English."
—Gillian Esquivia-Cohen, *Kenyon Review*

"A pointed critique of late capitalism incarnated in today's manipulative pharmaceutical industry, of rapid modernization in postcolonial contexts, and of facile arts. [*Ornamental*] showcases the impact of economic exploitation on the human body and desire, and probes the complicity of arts, architecture, philosophy, and language in capitalism's crooked dynamics. I read translated literature to connect with my linguistic others, to get out of my skin, and see the world through the eyes of those I may never meet otherwise. Cárdenas's novel and Davis's translation did just that for me. Davis has masterfully rewritten Cárdenas's novel in English." **—Sevinç Türkkan, *Hopscotch Translation***

THE DEVIL OF THE PROVINCES

THE DEVIL OF THE PROVINCES

JUAN CÁRDENAS

Translated by Lizzie Davis

COFFEE HOUSE PRESS
Minneapolis
2023

First English-language edition published 2023
Copyright © 2017 by Juan Cárdenas
Translation © 2023 by Lizzie Davis
Cover artwork © Tree Abraham
Cover design by Tree Abraham
Book design by Ann Sudmeier
Author photograph © Federico Ríos

First published by Editorial Periférica as *El diablo de las provincias,*
© 2017 by Juan Cárdenas c/o Indent Literary Agency
www.indentagency.com

Coffee House Press books are available to the trade through our primary distributor, Consortium Book Sales & Distribution, cbsd.com or (800) 283-3572. For personal orders, catalogs, or other information, write to info@coffeehousepress.org.

Coffee House Press is a nonprofit literary publishing house. Support from private foundations, corporate giving programs, government programs, and generous individuals helps make the publication of our books possible. We gratefully acknowledge their support in detail in the back of this book.

LIBRARY OF CONGRESS CATALOGING-IN-PUBLICATION DATA

Names: Cárdenas, Juan Sebastián, 1978– author. | Davis, Lizzie, 1993– translator.
Title: The devil of the provinces / Juan Cárdenas ; translated by Lizzie Davis.
Other titles: Diablo de las provincias. English
Description: First English-language edition. | Minneapolis : Coffee House Press, 2023. | Identifiers: LCCN 2022045974 (print) | LCCN 2022045975 (ebook) | ISBN 9781566896771 (paperback) | ISBN 9781566896788 (epub)
Subjects: LCGFT: Novels.
Classification: LCC PQ8180.413.A72 D53313 2023 (print) | LCC PQ8180.413.A72 (ebook) | DDC 863/.7—dc23/eng/20220923
LC record available at https://lccn.loc.gov/2022045974
LC ebook record available at https://lccn.loc.gov/2022045975

PRINTED IN THE UNITED STATES OF AMERICA

For Doctor Esperanza Cerón, my mother.

For my sisters, Alejandra and Juliana.

THE DEVIL OF THE PROVINCES

"Hands developed with terrible labor by apes /
Hang from the sleeves of evangelists."

—Robert Bly, "The Great Society"
from *The Light Around the Body*

"Or did we really get lost in the woods?"

—Enrique Lihn, "Hothouse" ("Invernadero")
from *The Dark Room and Other Poems,*
trans. Jonathan Cohen

"If you consent, neither you nor any other
human being shall ever see us again; I will go
to the vast wilds of South America. My food
is not that of man; I do not destroy the lamb
and the kid to glut my appetite; acorns and
berries afford me sufficient nourishment. My
companion will be of the same nature as myself
and will be content with the same fare. We shall
make our bed of dried leaves; the sun will shine
on us as on man and will ripen our food. The
picture I present to you is peaceful and human,
and you must feel that you could deny it only in
the wantonness of power and cruelty."

—Mary Shelley, *Frankenstein*

1.

Just when things were starting to look dire, a temporary job came up at the all-girls boarding school. The woman who ran the licensure program explained that there was some urgency, since the usual teacher would soon be taking parental leave. He did the math: the pay was bad, so were the hours, but by then, he had no choice. He'd just come back from fifteen years abroad, and it was clear within weeks—spent on the couch of a friend, right in the capital—that his foreign degrees did not in fact guarantee him a top-tier professorship. People like him, with the same credentials or better ones, had become vulgar goods. He resolved to lower his expectations, try his luck at the public college back home, stay with his mother awhile. He bought the cheapest plane ticket he could find and said good-bye to his friend, his only one left in the capital, one of a few in the world. They'd known each other since childhood and had dreamed even then of leaving behind the sclerosis of their small city, imagining distant countries. His friend asked if he was serious. Let me remind you, the place is a shithole. Don't rush into this, he said. Stay here as long as you need. The biologist shrugged and smiled so the other would understand that the small city, almost village, so conservative and backward that they had to make fun of it constantly just to exorcise the stigma of having been born there, had in the end worked out a way of turning the tables. I'm going, but don't think I'm proud of it, the biologist said, tragicomic: I give up, destiny wins—his friend laughed a scared animal's laughter. There was nothing else to be done. It was time to breathe through the wound, to smile without all that scorn, maybe even with a certain admiration: the provincial sense of humor had shown itself to be more than just that; it seemed it was also a minor determinist doctrine. Well, take care of yourself. And tell your mom I miss her, said his friend in the accent they shared. That's how they'd always talked to each other: aspirated consonants, knowing sarcasm, never putting on the affected *tú,* which everyone they grew up with used to conceal the *vos.* That slack southern dialect the biologist hadn't entirely lost, despite years of willing exile.

He'd been at his mother's a week when the boarding school called. A histrionic voice informed him that someone they trusted had put in a good word, and the biologist was left wondering who the unexpected benefactor might be. They had to say everything twice, not because he wasn't paying attention, but because he was struggling to absorb his new, albeit impermanent, life:

he was a substitute teacher now, biology and ecology, four courses at an all-girls school on the outskirts of the dwarf city.

A few days later, driving down the highway in a beat-up Mazda 323, as the morning sun revealed little by little the rippling of the coffee fields, the blue of the cordillera, he was filled with excitement, thinking for the first time that maybe he could get used to this place after all, could learn how to live here again. I'll adapt, he thought, smiling because of course that's the word that had come to him. But resistance kicked in almost instantly: this country is as cunning as the devil.

2.

On the campus, there were three buildings: one very large one, with three floors and a paved schoolyard; a smaller one, where the girls' rooms were; and a chapel. Everything was painted a verdant blue, which shimmered in the permanent humidity—the region was temperate, mountainous. In the exterior corridor where he was waiting for the director, the biologist noticed a shell-shaped niche that housed the Virgin Mary. The statue was humble, plaster-cast, unlikely to awaken anyone's fervor. Left to fend for herself in the wall, she fulfilled a dubious decorative role. The biologist didn't have time to guess at the reasons for her neglect, since just then the director showed up and summoned him into her office. She reiterated point-blank that the usual teacher was only on leave: this is temporary, she warned. She was frank about the money too, and the teaching load. She seemed like a resolute woman, one who never wasted time, and the biologist saw himself swept along by all her executive vigor, saying yes again and again, as if signing on to some colonial venture or research expedition.

They assigned him a desk in the teachers' lounge. Not the one that should have belonged to him, given that he was standing in as head lecturer—the young math teacher would sit there—but a smaller one, in front of a window facing the basketball court, a garden, and the barbed-wire fence of a pasture where two or three cows were grazing.

The first days were quiet, as he'd expected. The students behaved but showed little interest in what he was trying to teach them. They all dressed impeccably, uniforms ironed, hair styled one of three ways: down, pulled into a ponytail, or combed back and held in place with a modest headband. Under no circumstances were they to cut it short; dye, tease, or highlight it; or do anything else that might attract attention.

Most of the students came from towns in the south of the province, but there were also a few Black girls from the Pacific coast, probably daughters of public officials and local teachers, granted scholarships or financial aid. Only ten were from the dwarf city, and of those ten, half were pregnant.

A girl who was showing under her baggy uniform sweater interrupted him during a lecture on Darwinism. She asked if God had made it so every animal, every plant, had its own purpose. And the biologist, surprised by the girl's sudden interest but excited nonetheless at the prospect of teaching her something, launched into his explanation: Not necessarily; some traits do develop to serve a particular purpose, but there are also many cases when evolution would seem to entirely contradict reason and, therefore, design. In other words, nature invents things constantly, but most of what it invents is useless for millennia, and it's not unusual for an adaptation to atrophy or, alternatively, change its function. For example: the avocado. The avocado is an excellent example. The tree began to produce a fruit that tasted so good it caught the attention of large mammals known as gomphotheres, very much like elephants, mostly found in the forests of Central America. No animal today could digest a fruit with a pit of that size—but the gomphotheres could, thanks to their huge digestive tracts, which enabled the dispersal of the seeds. So the avocado wins, you might say, but the thing is, gomphotheres went extinct nearly two million years ago, and yet avocados go on existing, without even one discernible variation. It's as if they haven't realized there are no gomphotheres walking this earth, they think their evolutionary strategy works just fine, when the truth is, everything's changed, they're just completely oblivious to it—an avocado spends its whole life just waiting around for a ghost . . .

The biologist stopped short because the girl with the tip of a belly was staring at him as if he had lost his mind.

Thank you for that question, he said before carrying on with whatever was in the textbook. At one point, he turned to write something on the board and heard a playful murmur: So are paramo avocados for baby elephants? Some laughter, no cause for alarm. The class returned to normal, and he finished up his lecture without further interruptions.

The joke had to do with small avocados, about the size of plums, produced by forests at high elevations. Maybe that question was actually relevant, thought the biologist, smiling. At his tiny desk in the teachers' lounge, looking out at the empty basketball court, he dreamed about digging up fossils of shoebox-sized baby elephants.

3.

After work, he went to the grocery store with his mother. They filled the trunk of the Mazda with bags and talked on the way back about how the dwarf city had grown, the new buildings and developments, the progress, which, to his mother, was evident in the mathematical fact of two big malls rather than one, both always crowded with shoppers. Two, she said, her fingers like antennae, and they're building another one off the north exit. Then, gesturing toward new apartment towers to one side of the highway, she assured her son that things were much better now. We're really taking off, she said, and he gave her a tepid nod, though he had to admit that his mother was getting on well. There was a reason she'd managed the move to that new subdivision, where comfortable people lived, on either side of Batallón and right behind the runway—luckily, there were just one or two flights every day, plus maybe a prop plane, the kind people took to the coast. The biologist found the new house uninviting compared to the one where they'd lived before, in the city center. Its design was the result of a simple and mechanical application of several trends now afflicting the city, which made

him think of an old truism: that forms tend to repli-
cate in nature just as rampantly as they do in man-made
contexts, but with much truer aesthetic aim. In fact,
there wasn't one area in the whole house that the biologist found inviting, no niche that encouraged spiritually
enriching activity. The living room, the bedrooms, nothing enticed you to stay for long; the house seemed built of
only stairs and hallways, and the biologist could do nothing but wander from end to end, go up and come down,
out and in, open and close the fridge door, sometimes lie
in front of the TV. Pure actions, he thought, completely
devoid of intention. Yet another consequence of his
return to the role of son. Some nights, once his mother
was in bed, the biologist went outside to breathe in the
coolness, smoke a joint in an old rocker. Those were his
only moments of peace in that house: something inside
of him would release, and for a minute or two, joint
smoldering in his fingers, he could see how the tangle
of things—still palpitating and wet, freshly ground—
came to rest on the damp grass: the city a world away;
phrases in different languages; the curtains of the studio
where he lived for two years after the divorce; the over-
powering odor of spices and tallow wafting in through
the window onto the courtyard, saturating his clothes;
pieces of recent memory he tried to process and stretch
as if filling a strange meat casing with scraps, as desirous as

he was fearful that something whole might come of them all and grant meaning and solidity to the set. Because he suspected that in the end, the light, the soft sheen with which this or that memory surfaced, the imminence of a sweet fragrance that never arrived—there was a secret order threaded through it all, a directive that posed itself to him again and again. That was my life, was all he could say. That was my life, and everything went to shit. There's an economy to these things, even to the doling out of painful situations, like divorce. Failure, too, has its place in the equation. Professional failure, even romantic failure, is not a life sentence, really, because in time, with proper training, you end up overcoming it by brining yourself deep inside, just like an olive in vinegar. You kill time at the bar, you brood over and under platitudes with an old hand from some other shipwreck; with any luck, he'll impart some advice about how to ration state benefits, pump the brakes, so you can cultivate new vices even in poverty. Of course he was fully aware that the causes had been external: they'd made cuts across the sciences, his funding had dried up. The rest had been merely allowing himself to tumble over the edge, giving in to the inertia from the blow. But the biologist was convinced that in the subsequent fall, the slow and predictable sliding by of the cliff face, there lay hidden a secret about himself, about his most intimate structure, something that, in the end, had vested him with an identity and maybe even a style. I *am* that form of falling, he thought, inhaling whatever was left. That gesture—letting go—is essentially me. Then he'd flick away the last leg of the smoking insect, a jot of almost ash that died in the wet grass without a fight, swathed in the song of a thousand frogs. After that, he'd gradually recover a sense of his surroundings—he was back in the dwarf city, back on this side of the world, at his mother's house—and feel guilty over how generous she was being, how understanding. To the point of not having externalized a single sign of reproach, nothing that would make evident what he knew she was thinking deep down: that of her two sons, the elder one was the least equipped for this world. And oh, wasn't life cruel. Because to be perfectly honest, she'd have rather seen the biologist taken early and not her younger son, the apple of her eye, her pride and joy, her missing half. The life-giving avocado absent a father. Because that's how she had arranged it all in her head, but this world was so careless, so cruel, that it marred all she'd planned without planning, all she'd drawn up in the depths of her deepest sleep, on the blackboard of her heart. Which was: that the younger son should prevail over the elder. That the elder son was an outline, and the younger, the final draft. But life is cruel, so cruel, she said over and over, it's hard but unsteady too, and senseless, ruled by a geometry we'll never understand but that we feel in our very flesh, and when you formulate a plan, when you commit to an idea, and you sketch and forge and sculpt, life will take care of distorting it all, as if demons were running the show, lovers of twists and turns and never straight lines, mercurial satyrs, not God, God forgive me, sometimes I think that God lies in death and not life, because death is eternal rest, the perpetual light of righteousness. Life, on the other hand, all that we call nature, that's the devil's work, the devil sides with beasts, with snakes and scorpions. The devil makes his nest in the eye of a bird, an egg's speckled shell, a creatures' claws, a mess of feathers, the river's whirl.

4.

One morning, a very fine rain began falling upon the dwarf city, so fine it seemed less like rain and more like sweat springing up from the skin of things. Thick amber clouds came down from the mountains, marched in tight formation across the whole valley, paused above the runway, and finally dropped down onto the streets of the housing development. Through the small bathroom window, toothbrush in mouth, the biologist watched them blot out a row of houses, the neighbor's blue car, a guava tree that didn't yet feel like flowering, two children awaiting their school bus.

His mother usually slept in—they almost never crossed paths in the morning—but that day, she had an appointment, so they sat at the table together while a young Indigenous woman served them breakfast without speaking.

On the radio, they were talking about the highways going up all over the province, the many millions the central government had sown throughout the region. They'd brought on two guests from opposing political parties to discuss the future of oil and mining concessions. His mother was so transfixed that she let her coffee go cold. The biologist, however, couldn't detect a debate; the contenders proposed the same formulas, barely bothered to paraphrase; the only difference was tone. One of them wanted to seem at ease and open to discussion. The other was emphatic, unrestrained: his voice, from time to time, took on apocalyptic timbres. The mother clearly preferred the latter and egged him on by laughing and gleefully smacking the table. The biologist asked her who the hothead was. She ignored the insult and said he was a friend of hers, an entrepreneur; he's a horse breeder, in fact, and one of the few men I know who are called, really called, to turn this province around. Rushing his last sips, the biologist took in the radio voices twined like two snakes in the warm kitchen air: nervous, excited voices scouring words, always verging on shrill, two rhetorical modes well greased by the slippery tongue of the host.

The fog in the dwarf city didn't clear until well into morning. At the boarding school, it hung on even longer. A ray of sun bore through the clouds and made it all the way to a classroom, where the biologist was lecturing on the importance of native plants. The girls yawned. In the neighboring pasture, iguazas cackled. It was like the day had refused to start from the beginning: an attempt that erased with its elbow whatever it drew with its hand. A feint at a Friday determined, at whatever cost, to keep down the temporal spiral, just to be able to vomit it up in the night.

Later he found himself in the cafeteria, eating lunch with the young math teacher—the woman who'd stolen his desk—and a fat Black man who taught PE. The biologist felt as if they were subjecting him to some kind of interrogation. They wanted to know if his contract was temporary, was it true that he'd done all that research abroad; they asked questions as if a higher power had sanctioned them. He sidestepped every one, acting part distracted, part discreet. At some point, the man let slip that nearly every teacher at the school had been hired because someone called in a favor; he wanted to know who had backed the biologist. The question caught him off guard. The truth was, he had no idea who had recommended him, and just as he was preparing some vague reply, his mother's raging friend came to mind, the horse-breeding entrepreneur from the radio show. He opened and closed his mouth, tried to hide the obfuscation, and arrived at a grudging response: Nothing has ever been handed to me in my life. The math teacher shot him a smirk that struck him as overplayed. She must just be picking up sarcasm, he thought, she'll get the hang of it soon.

After lunch, the sky clouded over again. And just when they least expected it, a mighty downpour was unleashed, buckets of water falling on matted branches, flashes of lightning that, rather than hurl themselves down to earth, writhed uncomfortably in the sky and lit the nervous insides of dark clouds. The biologist couldn't stop thinking about the benefactor. He'd have to ask his mother, coax it out of her with her own artfulness, beat her at her own game. Of course, it was also possible his mother had nothing to do with it; there was always a small chance his luck was determined by more than just the microcosm of family, a thought that brought relief but also new anxieties.

He was robotic through his last classes. At one point, the girl with the tip of a belly raised her hand. Can we talk about avocados again? I've been wondering why the gomphotheres went extinct. Not today, the biologist said. She made another attempt: God has a plan for all of us, even the avocado. The biologist snorted, impatient, and carried on with his lesson.

5.

Night fell, and the streets of the dwarf city were still wet. The biologist went to a bar downtown, and there, among the pool tables, where he'd expected to find his dealer, was a woman who threw her arms around his neck. He smiled, confused, and returned the embrace, stalling to try to remember a name or a circumstance. His memory of the woman was pleasant, he could sense it. That's why he agreed to the exchange of shallow phrases, the repeated physical contact. Come have a drink with us, she said. And he, more curious than eager, let her take his arm and lead him to one of the pool tables, toward a large group of strangers. Someone put a beer in his hand while the woman explained that she'd started a production company in the capital. All the people around the pool table were her colleagues. Tomorrow we're going out to the hacienda, why don't you come with us? The biologist looked her in the eye to make sure she was serious, not just being polite. The last time he'd seen her was at his brother's wake, ten years earlier. I can't believe it, she kept saying, we haven't changed a bit, have we. You're a little skinnier, maybe, but other than that, identical—you haven't aged a day! The biologist smiled, looked away, and sipped on his beer. Someone told me you were back, she said, I don't remember who. It's true, I'm back, the biologist said, distracted because as the conversation went on, he kept remembering details. The woman had posed as his brother's girlfriend for years. A willing accomplice who'd served as a smoke screen so Mom's favorite son could hide his faggotry. Looking over at the pool players—hardly any women—he assumed she was one of the type who like to surround themselves with gay men. He knew almost nothing about her, though they'd met when they were teenagers, though they'd locked themselves in the bathroom to do lines off the toilet lid on the day of the wake.

That's when the dealer showed up and waved him across the bar. The biologist made his excuses. I've got to run, he said, and she repeated her invitation to spend the weekend down at the hacienda. I'll give you a ride, she said. Where are you staying? The biologist didn't answer. Don't worry about it, I'll drive. They said good-bye with a hug that she tried to prolong, maybe because of the memory of his brother, or the mess of feelings they'd shared that day in the bathroom, he wasn't sure. Had they done something other than cry and get high together? The biologist remembered her black dress, his hand on her black silk tights, her blond hair smeared with tears and running makeup. Thanks again for inviting me, I'll see you tomorrow, he said, those same images still cycling in his head. Her hair, the silk tights. Had he really touched her leg that way in the bathroom?

Beneath an enormous painting of various breeds of dogs playing pool, the dealer held out a soft, cool hand. Tosqué, he said, raising his eyebrows. All good?

6.

They sat down to smoke on a bench in the main plaza. His time with the dealer, who had long hair and went by one of those names he imagined people gave themselves in rough neighborhoods, was as close as he'd gotten to friendship since his return. I don't know if I'm getting too deep in too much shit or what, the dealer said, staring into the void. The plaza was quiet, pretty, hardly anyone out, and a glow like ancient dust was coming off the streetlights. I don't know what it is, he said, but lately, I've been showering in the dark. The biologist let out a yellowish puff and looked at him, surprised. In the dark? Yeah, I only shower lights-off now, I keep it pitch black, the dealer went on, I lock myself up in the bathroom and wait till the water's real hot so it almost burns. You should try it. It's scary at first, but then you catch on, you get used to it, and then it turns into a scene that's, I don't know, astral—I mean, it's heavy. The biologist let out a laugh. What are you, some kind of shaman now? Usually the dealer was immune to any teasing, but this time he'd wanted someone to take him seriously. He went quiet, stone faced, exhaled smoke so it would twist beneath the streetlights. Parce, all

due respect, but I don't think you get it, he said. Before, I'd
have the music turned all the way up. I sometimes even
danced. I could never do that now. Everything has to be
silent. You'll say it's because of the drugs, and sure, I'm
steady, there's no way around it, but this shower thing is
something else completely. It's on another level, bróster,
how do I put this, it's like I'm down in the huaca, stiffs
and gold and all that, I'm not messing. It's happening
inside me, it's deep—deep down as whirlpools or dead
people. Like I need some kind of change, need to do
something else, stop smoking so much, try at something.
The biologist rolled a joint and stood up. Come on, let's
walk, he said.

    In that state, stores closed, streets practically empty,
no traffic and no daytime clamor, the old city center
recovered something of its innermost beauty. Walking, at
this hour, was pleasant. Like being on a theater set where
colonial homes, baroque churches, the clock tower, the
small mansions, seemed to have grown tired of all their
seigneurial posturing. At night, resigned to granting a
picturesque scene to the passersby, the architecture had
an air of honorable defeat. It occurred to the biologist
that, absent the powers that called for their construction
and centuries-long conservation, the buildings stopped
signaling anything: the dwarf city's historic district was
no more than an empty husk, a magnet with no pole, a

signifier that only referenced itself—like an archaeo-
logical park full of stone gods no one feared anymore,
unexpectedly childish, practically playthings. His friend
appeared indifferent to the trace of romantic decline,
which he thought confirmed the theory, and which made
him wonder if his generation might be the last that could
recognize the flirtation. Because even here, the dealer,
several years younger, continued to ruminate on his
problems, his shower astral trips. Listen: you see things
in the dark, he said. Little lights show up, the shapes they
make are outrageous, like the shit you see in the ocean,
have you ever been to the ocean? I haven't, parce, not once.
The ocean scares me, bróster. But these shapes pop up like
spaceships and make their own light.

It had been days before the biologist figured out that
the dealer was calling him *bróster* and not the more standard *bróder,* probably because all across the city, restau-
rants were now selling broasted chicken, chicken battered
in crispiness, and the ads were large and vivid, and many fea-
tured chickens fresh from the fryer; or chickens dressed
up like waiters, in bowties; or a chicken winking and
pointing one thumb at a chicken dead on a platter. That
almost random approach to word choice seemed, to the
biologist, to echo the capriciousness of nature. He imagined the dealer's lexicon as an animal that had adapted to
survive any change in environment; capable of evolving,

even producing new organs if necessary; feeding, when it had to, on foreign tongues. And then he started to wonder about his own lexicon, the strange blend of accents in which there existed, in relative harmony, various word-stocks and tones and temperatures, amassed over two decades of willing exile, all resting on local cadences. Has my lexicon also evolved to survive any change in environment? What kind of bowlegged animal is it? Another idea, even more outlandish: perhaps his friendship with the dealer wasn't between two people but two languages instead, a spontaneous symbiosis completely disconnected from the will of the speakers who claimed them.

Just then they heard shouting across the way. A drunk man was lurching around in front of a government building. Sons of bitches! His cries filled the street. They're thieves, I tell you! They take us for all we're worth! Suck us dry like vampires! Bunch of bastards, they are. I said vampires! Come down here and show us how tough you really are, I'll take every one of you! The drunk, emboldened, picked up whatever he found on the street and hurled it against the colonial building's facade. Two policemen appeared and went over to calm him down, they exchanged words. They escorted him off in the end but never got violent. They did just enough to expel the drunk, and then the street returned to total calm. A calm that encouraged getting lost in one's thoughts, chance observations. They saw a giant moth on a white wall, one of those moths with wings that appear to have eyes. The biologist didn't know much about entomology, much less about lepidopterans—he'd specialized in bears and other large mammals—so he paid it little notice. The dealer, on the other hand, got very close to the moth and took a series of smiling selfies. At some point they tire of circling streetlights, and then they stay put till they die, the biologist said, uninterested. The dealer took one last photo, tongue sticking out so it looked like he was about to lick the moth. Nice, right? he said.

Later they went to a liquor store with tables in the back. That was their usual place—it was cheaper than getting drunk at any bar. They asked for aguardiente at the front and then went to the other side, which was packed. There were even some couples dancing. They took the last empty seats, two chairs shoved against a wall, and struck up a conversation with the group at the nearest table: three bank tellers, two city employees, and a guy who did delivery for a Chinese place. It was clear they were relaxed, their speech hot and viscous from booze. One of the tellers, the most conventionally attractive of the three, said, It's true what they tell you, this really is the happiest country on Earth. They almost all agreed, each for different reasons, but she maintained that the principal source of this happiness was faith: No

one here loses faith. Everyone's a believer, right up to the
very end. The dealer, who'd been feeling transcendent all
night, was gazing at her with the eyes of a devout child.
I'm crazy about América, he said, seductive, I'm as faithful as they come. I'm also inventing my own meditation
technique, and it has me on a whole other plane of real-
ity. The teller didn't give him the time of day. She was
more interested in the biologist, whom everyone at the
table was treating with a mixture of reserve and con-
descension, as often happens with outsiders. What do
you think, professor? the teller asked. Are we really in
the happiest country on Earth? The question surprised
the biologist, and he wound up enmeshed in a lecture
on the word *happiness*. If we don't know what happiness
is, we can't ever know if we're happy, he finished. And
the kid who delivered Chinese food stroked his chin
and said, That's really interesting. Then one of the city
employees, the only dissident, began railing against the
idea of happy and unhappy countries. Everybody shits,
he said, it's absurd to even think about doing a survey,
let alone rank every country. That's reckless spending
for you, and not just money, time too. I mean, what a
bunch of idiots, and we're even worse for sitting here
talking about them. Another teller, whose blond bangs
were shaped like a parasol, protested, still in high spirits:
But scientists did those surveys, they made calculations,

it's data! The misanthrope interrupted: Propaganda. Nobody's happy, the closest you can even get is content. And that's only if you don't know better—an animal doesn't care whose tit's in its mouth. The pretty teller kept insisting on the primacy of faith. The dealer zealously backed her. The biologist drank in silence, embarrassed he'd let slip a dissertation. Then the delivery guy had the fine idea of taking the third teller out for a dance, she was short and squat and hadn't said anything about anything, and that was enough to end the discussion of happiness, but not the discussion of faith.

The pretty teller asked the biologist if he'd said all those things because he was faithless, and the biologist admitted that was something he'd never asked himself. Maybe I am a believer and just haven't realized it yet, he said. The teller smiled with inexplicable tenderness and said, Without faith, all we are is pitiful little animals. Soon the delivery guy had attached himself to the fat teller. That seemed to encourage the dealer, who tried his luck with the teller with parasol bangs. The biologist, goaded on by the others, danced without wanting to, dragging himself through the steps with the pretty teller, repeatedly stumbling into the neighboring tables, though no one complained. That night, they were all semi-happy, semi-drunk, semi-lucid, everyone raising their glasses to the softened post-downpour humidity. And something in the biologist's body detected forces—who knows what kind—awakening in the dwarf city, as if a natural phenomenon no one had missed were quietly drawing closer, catastrophe not far behind. But unwilling to give in to superstition, he drove back the threat and kept smiling, shuffling his feet, semi-aroused by the pretty teller's movements.

7.

He dreamed he went back to the house in the city center, the old house where he and his brother grew up, a few blocks from the sciences building, on the street the biologist had managed to avoid since his arrival.

In the dream, though, he felt no fear. He came around the corner, almost running, and climbed into the house through a window, determined to find the keys to enter his house.

Everything was intact inside, exactly the same as before. He looked for the keys everywhere, rifled through drawers, stuck his head under every bed, even parted the amaranth leaves to check the dirt in the flowerpots since his uncle would sometimes hide things there. The house was empty. There was no one there he could ask where the house keys were. There were some in his pocket, but no: those were keys to someplace else, they opened other doors, not the door to his house. He gave up and drifted across the living room, stared out the window onto the street. I won't ever be able to leave this place, he thought as he watched people pass, one who resembled his brother, semi-hidden, semi-alive. The biologist leaned out for a better look. Yes, it was his brother, playing dumb; he didn't want to be seen among such strange people. The biologist finally understood what was going on: his brother had tricked him, and now they had traded places. He, and not his brother, was in the role of dead man. And without keys, without the right keys, he couldn't change anything back. That asshole got me, he thought. Now I'm stuck haunting this house for who knows how long.

His brother was lost in the rush of the crowd, carried along down the street, like anyone off to the sciences building. That faggot did this to me, he did this. The biologist was crying tears of rage but didn't want anyone outside the window to see, so he hid in the dark of the living room, crouching next to some furniture. There, he thought, he could weep and enghost himself, complete the metamorphosis, as his mother had wordlessly ordered years before. Until something on his face, tears or the tissue itself, began to burn.

He woke up little by little, still furious, sandpaper in his throat, and that's why it took him so long to notice the powerful stream of light coming through an unfamiliar window. That's what was making his face burn, not metamorphosis or tears. Next to him, the attractive teller was sleeping, and the biologist thought of fruit wrapped in newspaper, ripening overnight.

Deftly, he got out of bed and dressed without waking the woman, who was even more beautiful sleeping than awake. He left the room on tiptoe, the rest of the place coming back to him: a small apartment in one of those public-housing blocks now scattered all over the country, same as any monocrop. Through the living-room window, he saw the new street, freshly paved; other identical buildings; a few small tin houses they'd likely raze soon to make room for more apartments; and at the end, an enormous pasture. That's it, the biologist thought, the knife-edge of the dwarf city, and he sipped water that tasted of rusted metal and glue. By then he'd already forgotten his dream entirely, but the feelings of horror and unease hadn't yet cleared. The biologist attributed them to the hangover, and his head emptied like a cracked jug while he tried to peel a sticker from the window with his nail. "Jesus Is the Way," it said. Underneath, in smaller letters, "The Prince of Peace."

He left the apartment without saying good-bye to the teller.

It's better that way, he thought later, at the bus stop next to a woman with a basket of granadillas de quijos. The woman mistook the biologist's curiosity for hunger and offered him fruit. Take one, she said, you can try one for free. The biologist ended up buying a dozen, and by the time the bus showed up, he'd eaten four. Delicious, he said, like flowers in the flesh. *Passiflora popenovii.* The woman didn't understand the Latin, but she must have connected it with religion, because she hurried to explain that granadillas de quijos were the true fruit of the Garden of Eden. What Adam and Eve ate right before getting kicked out. The last little bite of happiness. Well, the last and the first, the woman said, and they laughed.

It was a perfect day, blue sky and a few pure-white clouds fraying bit by bit over a landscape of new buildings and empty pastures.

8.

Actually, the biologist thought later, on the way to his friend's hacienda, there is a religious allusion in the genus *Passiflora:* Jesuit missionaries came up with it back in the seventeenth century, sure that they saw, in the climbing plant's flowers, the instruments of the Passion: the nails, the whip, the crown of thorns. From *Passiflora,* of course, came *passionfruit.* And in an unavoidable link in the chain of associations, the biologist thought of his uncle, his mother's brother, the first person to tell him the story of the Jesuits and the flower. When the biologist and his brother were kids, the uncle kept up a small plot just outside the dwarf city, walking distance from lots that have since, no surprise, been colonized by new buildings. On that land, their uncle had grown potatoes, tomatoes, lulos, guayabos, guamas, and several species of *Passiflora,* or, as he always called it, passionflower. This is not a garden, their uncle would say, it's a finely tuned system for luring animals. And of course, that's what it was. Every day, depending on the hour, dozens of flying creatures—birds, insects, bats—gathered at the plot to feed on fruits and flowers. But it was the birds that their uncle cared

most about, swifts and hummingbirds especially, many
species of which could be found in the mountains
around the dwarf city: red-tailed comet, ruby-throated,
purple-crowned fairy, hermit, sword-billed, lyre-tailed,
blue-bearded, racket-tailed, they came by the dozens, not
just because of the flowers but also because of the water
dispensers their uncle had rigged up on the biggest
branches. The biologist and his brother sometimes spent
hours watching the little birds pirouette, registering each
sound, from near supersonic whistling to the most elabo-
rate calls, which the biologist, eyes closed, imagined as an
almost imperceptible sonic mille-feuille, layers of atonal
whirring slipped between consonants, r's and z's and f's,
harmony and percussion compressed in a single musi-
cal capsule. A miniaturized symphony that would vanish
with no promise of return, so all you could do was lie back
in a hammock and wait. A subtle, humble performance,
but no less demanding for it: they had to enlist all their
senses, had to reach a state of heightened concentration.
Eye ready to hunt fleeting colors. Ear attuned to the tiniest
music, which didn't always coincide with image. An excess
of minor stimuli would often disperse their attention, so
the exercise called for tact, patience, delicacy. Their concentration was no longer aimed at any one object, any one
target; instead, they perceived all at once and with equal
intensity various sources of movement, color, and sound,

without any idea where they might spring up—a dance no one had choreographed but which birds did to show the children *yes,* there was a guiding secret, a hidden weft that coordinated their movements. There must be some kind of order, the brother said once from his hammock. Maybe they take it in turns and we just can't tell.

In the Mazda, on a dusty road that crossed a cane plantation, the biologist was overcome with gratitude for his uncle, the family outcast, the man who failed at every project he attempted, the unrepentant dreamer who got tangled up in politics and arrested. I owe you, old man, he murmured over the radio voices. After all, it was his uncle who'd first spoken to him of Humboldt, who spent a day or two in the dwarf city en route to Quito to climb Chimborazo, and also of Bonpland, and Caldas, the local scientist and subversive whom royalist forces had put to death by firing squad—the main plaza in the dwarf city was named for him—stories that eventually delivered him to his calling as a naturalist. You're not a real Américan unless you're a naturalist too, his uncle would say. With that gratitude, there came a pang of guilt: since his return, the biologist hadn't once gone to visit his uncle, mostly because he was now in a group home, and he found those places depressing. That's when, for the first time, the biologist could sense that he was avoiding something, not a confrontation or epiphany, but something almost self-evident. I can't even walk down our street, he thought, much less visit the house. I'm a coward, that's what it is. But he still couldn't get to the root of his fear. What am I so afraid of? My brother? My mother? The living, or the dead?

Then the thoughts broke off because he was pulling up to the hacienda already, and from that moment on, the faculties bent on solving the family riddle were compelled instead to delve into the costumbrista watercolor before him: the old brick entry gate, little stone path, sprawling two-story colonial house; the palms and giant rain trees that opened their branches, guardian gods of the lawn out front.

9.

His friend didn't come out to welcome him, nor did anyone else, and as if in a dream, the biologist staggered past the old stables, now transformed into parking; walked the full length of the mute facade; and loitered near some rosebushes in the front garden. Then he stopped to look around, rotating on his own axis, and, almost giddy from the sound of a nearby stream, a sound he wouldn't consciously register for some time, he chose to settle at the foot of a zapote, stroke the grass with an open hand, confirm that he and this paradise had really overlapped in space and time. Incredible, he thought. Makes you never want to leave. On the ground was fruit birds had pecked at, and caravans of ants came and went through the holes in the rotten flesh.

He heard human voices in the distance, and that's when he finally noticed the sound of the stream, or rather, the current that had been tamed to encircle the property in parentheses. The noise of those happy voices echoed inside the house, and he allowed himself to be drawn toward what the setting was holding out to him: a state of mummified bliss. How charming, perfect, really, the biologist said out loud, as if in a dream or a nineteenth-century novel.

He watched two Black men come out of the house, both very handsome, both dressed in expensive, anachronistic clothing. They didn't see him since he was still crouching. The biologist jumped up and, after a moment's hesitation, lifted one hand in greeting, but the men had already passed, shrieking with laughter.

To him, or maybe the teenager still within him, the region's haciendas had always represented something like the pinnacle of normalcy: its most accomplished work. Given that he and his brother were sons of a single mother, given their uncle's standing as an ex-convict, given that they hadn't the slightest idea who their father was and their plebeian ancestors had lived for generations crammed into a shabby old house in the center of the dwarf city, to the biologist, the hacienda seemed to embody the opposite, i.e., family, respectability, productivity, tradition, a good name. The front side on the back of which his entire life had transpired. Now, of course, he knew more, and knew better. But that hadn't subtracted even one speck of the hacienda's magic. There's no question, he thought, the symbolism is masterful.

He walked toward the door the two men had come out of and saw a room filled with period furniture, portraits of the region's most prominent figures, porcelain ewers, all of it cordoned off like in a museum so curious people like him wouldn't touch or stumble into the artifacts.

He crossed from one end of the room to the other, looking for a hallway. Everything was just as it always had been; every object undisturbed, in its rightful place; plants, trinkets, pieces of furniture: a perpetual simulation of old La Caucana Arcadia.

Then he heard new voices, lots of them, and realized they were coming from the kitchen at the very back of the house. His friend jumped like she'd spotted a ghost when she saw him in the doorway, but she smiled to overwrite it and threw herself at him again, I can't believe you made it, it's so good to see you again, come over here and let me introduce you. So began a round of introductions, and the biologist, somewhat overwhelmed and with his guard up, started examining faces as if classifying a population of apes. They were all from the entertainment world, which, to him, implied every kind of conceit, from effervescent inanity to unwarranted arrogance, false humility somewhere in the middle. He settled near his friend in a corner of the kitchen, leaned back against the counter, and tried to relax and find his place in the group, as any primate would under the circumstances. It wasn't long before he'd finished taking stock. His friend, the producer and host, was working on a new project, a

telenovela set in the era of slavery, and she'd summoned
her trusted colleagues, potential actors included, to talk
about the screenplay and production. They were far into
the process and had already signed on a premier director.
Those were the words they insisted on using when they
described the creative genius, the man behind the whole
project: *a premier director.*

At first, the biologist followed the conversation from
a safe distance, but his researcher's curiosity gradually
urged him in. The idea was to do a show set in 1848,
just before José Hilario López, who'd backed emancipation, was voted in. The screenwriters had consulted with
several historians. The hook, of course, was the doomed
romance between an enslaved man and the hacienda's
mistress. And that love story was to be threaded with
subplots: diabolical mixed-race foremen, abuses of power,
free towns settled by runaways, tensions among hacenda-
dos who opposed emancipation and restitution. Politics
heating up romance, romance heating up politics, said
one screenwriter, a round little man in glasses. All morning, they'd been deep in discussion of how to portray the
enslaved, and they were waiting for the director to show
up and help them resolve the issues of race, sex, historical
accuracy, verisimilitude. They would mostly be filming
at that very hacienda, infamous throughout the region
for having enslaved thousands of men and women in its

plantation days. But the production team had also compiled a number of comparable literary and audiovisual references linked to the themes they hoped to explore. It's a genre, that's for sure, the other screenwriter said, adjusting his baseball cap. A genre unto itself. What should we call it? Plantation drama? Everyone gave the white man their full attention. Well, it doesn't really matter what we call it, it's a genre, and that means it has its own canon: *María, La mansión de Araucaima, Azúcar, Carne de tu carne, Casa-Grande e Senzala, Doña Bárbara,* some Machado de Assis, some Aluísio Azevedo, *Song of the South* . . . A Black woman interrupted him. Sorry, did you just say *Song of the South*? The Disney movie? The man in the baseball cap gave her a cautious look. Yes, he said, that's the one. The Black woman, the show's coproducer, was livid. You've got to be fucking kidding me. You're really going to sit here and tell me that racist agitprop is canonical? Let's get this out of the way: we will *not* be using *Song of the South* as a reference, end of story. The biologist's friend had to intervene to keep the conversation from devolving, as it had earlier, into accusations of racism and colonialism from all sides of the group.

The only ones who seemed to hover above the tension were the dandies the biologist had seen leaving, who burst back into the kitchen in the same festive mood as before, at which point everyone seemed to relax. Humor, said the host, humor is something we haven't talked about much, and I think it's important we don't neglect it. If there's one thing that takes a Colombian telenovela from good to great—and obviously I'm talking about the golden age, the eighties, that's the ethos we're after—if there's one thing that sets those telenovelas apart, it's got to be humor. Clever leads everyone can root for, situations so absurd they're almost surreal. That's something I'll need to see in your work, she said, turning to the screenwriters. Good jokes, a whole lot of humor, real mouthy characters. This isn't some magnum opus, and it's not a tragedy either. This is a show for everyone, for the most erudite Bogotano *and* the hired help.

The screenwriter in the baseball cap said, Sure, Colombian TV wasn't bad in the eighties, those shows took costumbrismo and did something new with it, even worked in some Italian neorealism, but these days, the series reigns, it's the saga of this century, and that's where we should go for our plotlines and our characters and our dialogue, so we can really firm up the genre. But yes, it should go without saying that this show needs to be for everyone—every class, every race, every creed. The stocky man in glasses, whom the biologist had identified as baseball cap's faithful squire, said he'd like to cross-breed today's sagas with eighties TV. And maybe it'd be smart for us to see what the gringos are doing, he said, how they're dealing with slavery, racial polemics, and go from there. Adapt that to our own history, instead of sitting here bickering.

The Black coproducer looked at the floor, biting her lip with barely concealed impatience, but said nothing.

The biologist was still feeling the effects of the previous night's binge. He couldn't open his mouth, in part because he had no strong opinions about TV or narrative style—topics in which he took little, if any, interest—but mostly because he had no idea what he was doing there, why his friend had invited him, what his role in this argument was.

Strangest of all, by then, his silence had turned uncomfortable for the others, who must have been asking themselves the same questions. But the host seemed to be enjoying the confusion, as if her friend's illegible presence were a show of some kind of power over everyone else in the room.

They spent the rest of the afternoon on the refurbished side of the property, swimming in the pool, drinking beer, playing table tennis, and dancing.

The biologist remained in that same state of semi-presence, trying not to stray too far from his friend and her coproducer, the only person there who asked him questions with genuine interest. The woman had a strange name the biologist forgot two seconds after he'd heard it, a name he assumed was one she had given herself. But the erasure of that name stayed with him for several minutes, a tablet effervescing in his body.

At one point in their conversation, the coproducer asked where he was teaching, and the moment he said the name of the place, she recoiled. Uy, she said, that must be tough. The biologist squinted, surprised. I mean because of the girls, she added. He still didn't understand. Nobody told you? The killings a few months back? Two girls, fourteen-year-olds . . . The blood drained from his face and his shoulders shrank, all the hairs on his back stood on end. No, the biologist said. I had no idea.

10.

That night they dined outside, at a table in the front garden, underneath the branches of the rain tree. They had seated the biologist on the same end as the coproducer, his friend, and her older sister, a woman who had aged early and who seemed to demand the entire party's attention each time she spoke. But the table was too long, so the conversation fragmented arbitrarily. The biologist observed the grande dame with morbid curiosity. It wasn't the first time he'd seen her, but he'd never before had the chance to sit so close to her personage, and she talked and talked as if in front of a camera. Over the course of the last fifteen years, while the biologist was away, that woman had made a stunning career in politics, and he was enthralled but also repelled by her. She had shown up unannounced, flanked by bodyguards, wheedling, and she sat at the head of the table, giving orders to no one in particular. The director will sit here, she commanded, waving a finger adorned with sparkling emeralds. The biologist's friend, who was clearly annoyed by her older sister's intrusion, replied coolly that the director hadn't arrived yet, but yes, they could leave that seat open, he'd

turn up soon, she was sure. He'll be here any minute,
the coproducer said, in the tone a sensible person uses to
calm an animal. He better be, the grande dame replied,
he better be, and having tasted nothing, she pushed away
her plate with one long fingernail. Then she started to
ramble on, nonsense about a pyramid they'd discovered
in Antarctica, thanks to the melting ice caps. It came up
in a documentary I was watching the other day. Did anyone else see that one? A pyramid, she said, a *pyr-a-mid,*
made by some ancient civilization, most likely extraterrestrial. Evidence of alien life in prehistory—they can't
hide it anymore. Then she crossed herself three times at
top speed, blurring the lines of the shape. Who can deny
the evidence, no one, no one, but God help us. It makes
you wonder, doesn't it? Are we descendants of apes or
aliens? The biologist cut in, joking that maybe the thing
they should worry about wasn't so much the pyramid but
the melting polar ice caps. The woman shot him a look,
her stunned face inlaid with a pucker, and extended one
bejeweled hand: a glitzed-up paw and a lot, a lot, of per-
fume, so much it made him dizzy. And this man is who?
Her eyes fluttered up and down the length of the table.
The biologist's friend explained. Ah, the old woman said,
showing her teeth. Your sweet little boyfriend's brother,
practically family, then. We've met before, haven't we?
Of course, the biologist said, taking her hand with open

repugnance. How could I forget, señora. That's right, I remember, the grande dame lied, now let's get one thing straight: this climate-change nonsense, it's no more than a leftist charade. Scientific terrorism. All the Lord's work is perfection, so the planet has a thermostat, it regulates its own temperature. Just think about freezers. You defrost them every so often, right? So they keep working properly. If you let the ice and the frost build up, that's when you're really in trouble. So what do you do? You defrost every once in a while, son, it's God's miracle cure, case closed. And that's the phase we're in now. Comes around every twelve thousand years, just like clockwork. So of course we're seeing traces of ancient civilizations in what we now know as Antarctica, because it used to be, twelve thousand years ago, tropical paradise, just like the one we're living in, and the people who lived there were really ahead of their time, thanks to the extraterrestrials.

The biologist couldn't help but let out a little laugh of sincere amusement, and the grande dame, unconcerned, carried on with her lecture. There's a pastor in our congregation, very bright, he's got his doctorate and everything—in other words, the kid is a true Knight of Faith. Well, he also happens to know quite a bit about science, and he explains everything, crystal clear. He thinks all this fuss is ridiculous, how could you blame

him? God is no amateur, no sir! Everything on this earth
of His runs like clockwork, I'm telling you.

Then the grande dame stood up, because the director had just appeared, and all the dinner guests stopped
doing what they were doing in order to greet him. Dear,
what a pleasure, said the señora, reextending the paw as
she stamped both his cheeks with a kiss. The director
bowed, an odd gesture, so solemn it seemed like mockery.
The pleasure is mine, señora, he said, Hello, everyone. He
sat down, and his orotund manner instantly made the
chair small. Next to him, right at the apex of the table,
sat a tall bald man who the biologist thought had an air
of true elegance. Every so often the director would whisper in his ear, and his expression would barely shift. He
was one of those people who smiled more with his eyes
than his mouth.

The director spent the rest of the dinner murmur-
ing to his friend's cousin, to the annoyance of the lady
with the ring, who went to great lengths to recapture
his attention and even took a call, practically shouting
so everyone would hear. This province and the one next
door at her mercy. All the Gran Cauca right in the palm
of her hand.

The director's subtle scorn eventually subdued her,
and she decided to retire to her quarters. She said good-
bye, performing another scene, kiss here, squeeze of a

shoulder there, and knocked over two glasses of wine in a clumsy turn of her huge ass. The liquid soaked the biologist's roasted potatoes. He pushed back his plate and said nothing so as not to prolong the farewell.

As she was walking away, the biologist noticed her mismatched shoes, each of a different style and color.

Can I ask you something? he said to his friend, who held up her hand to stop him. I already know what you're going to say, she said, I've been thinking about it all night. The biologist smiled, thinking they would now laugh together about the old witch's shoes, but his friend looked down, ashamed: You noticed too, she said through her teeth. There's not a single white person on the waitstaff.

11.

Around midnight, the dinner turned into a party. Little by little, the orthodox dancing came to more closely resemble the coupling of apes. People got high in the bathroom in twos and threes, and bands of cheerful drunks were all around. In one of them stood the biologist and the coproducer, surrounded by bit-part actors and impresarios. Because they were already drunk, the conversation went everywhere. The coproducer was decrying *Song of the South,* the Disney movie the screenwriter had praised earlier. It bothered her that the animals talked like Black people, especially the rabbit. And worst of all was the way it depicted the master-slave relationship, how they made it look so harmonious, so idyllic, like the natural order of things—Black folk off to the fields, so happy they can't help but sing. It's sickening, she went on, stomping a foot with so much conviction that no one dared disagree. Except for the biologist, who didn't want to say anything but kept thinking about the movie, which had been one of his childhood favorites. Over and over, he and his brother had rented it from their neighborhood videoclub. Over and over, they'd delighted in its songs, in the cross between live action and animation, in the friendship between a child whose parents divorced and an ex-slave named Uncle Remus—a griot, really, an oral historian; he knew all the tales a kid could ever want. For a minute, the biologist could feel the genuine mystery, the aura that shone around Remus each time he started talking about Br'er Rabbit. The camera closed in on his face, on his bulging eyes, and the children listened, enraptured: It happened on one of those zip-a-dee-doo-dah days, when the critters were closer to the folks, and the folks, they were closer to the critters, and if you'll excuse me for saying so, it was better all around. With that said, Uncle Remus opens his mouth to sing, and the moment he does, a bubble of colors explodes around his head, and then he's strolling through an enchanted world, cartoon creatures singing the refrain, Mister Bluebird is perched on his shoulder, all sweetness and satisfaction. And a little farther on, a buzzing bee dances on his finger, and Uncle Remus's eyes grow wider still, the eyes of an unsound mind, eyes in which, in his memory, the biologist now recognizes the trauma the fable shelters, eyes that watch the bee do her vernal dance on the ex-slave's finger while he sings: zum-zum-zum-zum-zum.

Sure, the film is racist, thought the biologist, but there's something transcendent to Baskett's performance of Uncle Remus, which contains an entire traumatic history.

Wasn't it set in the time just after the Civil War? During Reconstruction, when slavery had been abolished and Uncle Remus was stuck in limbo between two realities, one newly dead and the other still unborn? Uncle Remus is crazy. He sees birds that sing with the dulcet voices of women; he talks to a rabbit, to trees; everything around him—paths and rivers, hedgerows—quakes with impossible color. It's the story of a Black man driven mad by the limbo of history, thought the biologist. Everything else, the white child, his parents' divorce, the plantation, the willing servitude, it's all peripheral to his performance. You have to focus on Remus, shipwrecked by history, and his delusions.

The biologist thought it best not to share those indulgences in the company of the coproducer, whose stomping had cowed them all. He said he needed another drink and left the group.

On his way back from the bar, he crossed paths with his friend, who didn't seem as drunk as all the others. Come on, she said, grabbing his hand. The biologist let her lead him, holding on to his whiskey. That's just how he was: he let anyone pull him along if they pulled with enough conviction.

They crossed the garden, the patio, the entirety of the party; went through a side door into the old hacienda house; walked halls lit by lamps that gave off light like melted butter; made their way through the dark rooms blindly but avoided any objects, since his friend could have done it with her eyes closed; wound through salons where he barely made out the glint of porcelain, the lifeless gold of the picture frames. They went up a set of stairs that fed into a hallway and stopped in front of a door. There's someone here who's waited days to see you, said his friend. She pushed open the door and let him through before backing away discreetly.

Inside, in the middle of a room on its way to becoming a set, surrounded by shelves of fake books and imitation antiques, a woman was waiting for him on a velvet-upholstered settee. The light was weak, and the biologist had to get closer to see her face. He started shaking, his stomach turned. He tried to speak but couldn't. She, on the other hand, looked at him with her eyes open wide, an odd look of pride or nervousness on her face, lips twisted into an uneven shape the biologist knew well.

The woman motioned for him to sit next to her. For minutes, they didn't speak, just examined each other's faces, then she smiled tenderly and said: I wrote and you didn't answer. They both laughed because the reproach came fifteen years late. I'm sorry, said the biologist, I didn't know what to say. They laughed again, made incredulous by the encounter, which seemed even more unreal in a room filled with props. Ah, she said suddenly, before we talk about anything else, there's something I need to show you. Then she stood and, slightly unsteady, started to walk in circles. Right away the biologist noticed the unnatural rigidity in one leg. The woman rapped her knuckles against her thigh a few times. The biologist didn't know if he should stop smiling. None of it seemed believable yet, and for a second, he, too, felt shipwrecked by history, enveloped in a world delirious with color and papier-mâché, a mixture of dead things and living ones. It's a prosthesis, she said. Do you like it? He couldn't speak, couldn't move, couldn't take it all in. A prosthesis? he finally said. Yes, she replied, but a nice one. You better not be imagining one of those peg legs.

The biologist was speechless. Too much to absorb in too little time. Here he was with the high-school girl-friend he'd not seen in fifteen years, the first woman he'd ever loved, with whom he'd shared a time in his life that still felt fundamental to his trajectory. What was she doing at this hacienda? Why had his friend been the one to arrange their meeting? And more important than any of that, how did she end up with a prosthesis? How had she lost her leg?

It was easy for her to read the unease on his face, and she got out in front of it: We'll have plenty of time to catch up, she said. We'll just have to go piece by piece. First, let's talk about work.

12.

By the time he'd settled into the plastic pool chair the next morning, the biologist had made up his mind: he would leave the school and accept his first girlfriend's job offer. I've got nothing to lose, he thought. It'd be worse if I stayed on, at the mercy of those monsters. And the thing about the killings, could that possibly be true? I wouldn't last another month in that job.

The air smelled slightly sweet, and the biologist remembered how in the night, after saying good-bye to the woman with the prosthesis, just before getting in bed, he had seen the cane field burning through the window. Now, on the surface of the pool, there was a fine layer of ash and sugarcane bagasse. The dust formed thick swirls and slow knots, which the biologist, behind his dark glasses, watched evolve like primordial soup.

Many years before, that woman, his ex-girlfriend, had written the biologist some letters, right at the end of the era when people still sent them, when the two of them were just starting their biology degrees. One might have called them good-bye letters, good-bye to the past they'd shared, good-bye to a world disappearing before their eyes, but also good-bye to writing shaped by the rules of the post, interminable waiting, misconstrued addresses, returns to sender—the end of letters that traveled across half the world and were sometimes lost on the way; in a sense, the end of a kind of risk, of writing with the knowledge that the envelope was vulnerable to all sorts of unforeseen mishaps and, for precisely that reason, going about it in a very particular way, trembling but also trusting, which transformed the words completely: intention, style, form.

In the first, mailed from the dwarf city to a country across the Atlantic, the woman, back then still a teenager, told the biologist that she missed him, since he'd left she could barely get by, she was crazy about him, and not even the study of natural science could blunt the pain he'd left her with.

In the second, she tried out a theory presenting biology as both hard science and pathway to spiritual understanding, then she confessed she was dating one of her classmates. But I don't like him, not even a little. I'm just lonely. And I don't know how else to erase you, she said.

A few months went by before the third, which she wrote from the hospital. In that one, she told him about the accident, sparing no detail. Her tone was almost forensic, stripped of the melodrama that tinted the other letters, maybe under the influence of the brutality of the facts: they had amputated her leg, her body would be transformed from that moment on. There was no room for emotional blackmail or nostalgia, everything seemed too horrifying, too real, and all she was able to do was recount what had happened, more to arrange it into an order than to make sense of it: they were driving on the highway—she and her new boyfriend, the loyal, lovestruck classmate—on their way back from a party at the country club. She admitted they'd both had more to drink than they should have. When they were about to cross over the river, the boyfriend lost control, no one knew how or why, the car swerved, rear tires skidding, they spun in one direction then the other, and then there was no way out of it: they were struck by an oncoming vehicle. The cars collided with enough force to destroy the guardrail, they flew through the air, spinning like tops. But nobody's really witness to an accident, said the letter, allowing for some reflection. No one can access the facts. I was there, and not even I can say I experienced it. An accident like that doesn't happen to anyone. There are no subjects. Only objects. Noise made by matter, catastrophe, shit, noise made by bone, encephalic mass, twisted iron, gasoline, burning rubber, shapeless meteors making somersaults through the air, and then, having completed the requisite parabola, shattering the surface of the river, which at that time of year is higher because of the rains, and then one more noise, shattered water swallowing up all the noises, then nothing.

That was the only thing she could remember with any clarity, any awareness: the vacuum under the water, river flowing parallel to life, a subaquatic scene, maybe imagined, in which someone helped her out through a window after pulling her from the iron seizing her leg.

Then nothing. Until she woke up in the hospital, one leg missing.

The third letter also described the details of her recovery, operations, the doctors' vain attempts to save the limb, the amputation. It's too soon to know how all this is going to change me, she wrote. There's no telling how deep the roots of a severed leg go.

That third letter got lost in the mail, so the biologist never knew about the accident.

All that, they had pieced together the night before, on the velvet settee, feigning a clinical coldness like people dissecting a treasured pet.

Now the biologist, stretched out in the pool chair, watching the ash from burned cane cover the water's surface in arabesques, reviewed their conversation. Anyway, she had said, you wouldn't have written back. The biologist had thought about how to respond, wanting to be honest, wanting to show himself worthy of all she had shared. I don't know, he finally said, I was trying to change my life, I wanted to leave and never come back, but if I'd found out about the accident, who knows what I would have done.

After that, they sat quietly for a while, sensing it wouldn't serve them to go any further, and for a few seconds, they looked around, stunned. All the false objects, the room that would soon be the set of a telenovela.

Of course, they also talked about work.

His old girlfriend was running a study on the palm weevil, the scourge of the African palm, or the oil palm; a real headache for the agricultural sector. The biologist had never heard of that species, but the woman said enough for him to get a sense of the problem. Palm monoculture—a scourge in itself—had become widespread along the Pacific coast during the last decade and a half, and had created an ecosystem ideal for the propagation of the weevil, a coleoptera native to Asia that lays its eggs in palm sheaths. That animal's larvae feed on the fibrous heart of the host plant for the entire phase leading up to pupae formation, at which point they undergo their metamorphosis into adults, technically known as imagoes—the last developmental stage of an insect, after its final ecdysis.

The shocking numbers of larvae, and their voraciousness, took quite a toll on the palms, which yellowed and stopped producing fruit until they died, and that led to losses in the millions. Up until now, the best method for controlling them, besides preventive logging and ento-mopathogenic fungi, was to capture the males by luring them with pheromones, tricking them into believing that they were pursuing females when really, they were about to be entrapped in plastic jars. But recently the plague had intensified, the traps had quit yielding results, and the weevil wasn't stopping at just the oil palm, it was overwhelming other species too, like the peach palm and the palmetto.

The ex-girlfriend said that, according to the team's findings, the pheromone used in the traps was no longer effective; in a kind of adaptive miracle, the females had started modulating the chemical frequencies of their attractants. The biologist liked the metaphor, which made him think of pheromones as radio waves the females controlled to send messages. Now that man had successfully seized one band of frequencies, the females had arranged to transmit from others so the weevils could continue their campaign for domination, unstoppable.

Which is where you come in, the ex-girlfriend said. I know you know nothing about insects, I know that. They're not your specialty. But you did your whole disser-tation on pheromones and bears. Pheromones are phero-mones. We need you. You're brilliant at biochemistry. And that's pretty rare around here.

13.

Several pool chairs down, unaware that the biologist was half listening, the two screenwriters settled in and started griping about their bosses. One's Black, they're both gay, we can kiss good-bye any chance we had of making real TV. You're telling me. This is hell. The two of them ordering us around? What are they so upset about? You give them a little power and women like that, they're impossible. That's when they stopped short, because the one in the baseball cap had noticed the biologist, still as a caiman.

Flustered and trying to hide it, the screenwriter with glasses got in the water and splashed around clumsily, thinning the layer of ash on the unfazed blue of the pool. By the time he was back at the edge, the surface was totally clean, not a trace of the eddying dust.

What, hungover? the biologist called. The screenwriter with glasses was toweling off and let the other respond.

The biologist laughed imperceptibly. Or so he thought, until the one with the towel shot him a threatening look.

Just then the rest of the hungover swimmers showed up, and the tension was wrapped up in other conversations and then smothered.

The biologist remained motionless, always behind his dark glasses, attention trained on the future. And the future, under a sun that poured down on him like boiling lemonade, with the voices lulling him almost to sleep, the future was a single-file line of disjointed images: weevil, prosthesis, passionfruit broken in half, two elegant Black men walking arm in arm—where are those dapper men off to? He follows. As he suspected, they're headed nowhere in particular, they're misprogrammed robots, thinks the biologist, half-asleep, they go here and there and always say the same things, the same five set phrases, just like computers with viruses, and then they part ways, every man for himself; the biologist has to decide whom to follow and opts for the taller one, who walks with greater vigor than the other; more timid, that's the biologist, he lets himself come after if someone's resolutely out ahead. The man, slim and impeccably dressed, leaves the old hacienda, crosses into the newer part of the building, passes the pool, the biologist's deck chair, the biologist follows behind at a prudent distance, and the man, in his metallic blue suit, advances into the cane field, which, under the sour sun, at this windless hour, scatters a brightness utterly stripped of excitement, accustomed as it is to presiding over the landscape, sunk in that air of moral defeat that clings to the ever-winners. The metallic-blue suit disappears into green canes. The biologist follows.

But once he's inside the monocrop, there is no trace of the Black man. The monocrop denies time, the monocrop cancels it out. For the monocrop, there is no history and no human, only eternity, absolute void. The monocrop is God's will on Earth. An Earth without earth. A blessed algorithm that sums everything to zero for the greater glory of One. The biologist slips off into the timeless cane—another, larger shipwreck, one linked to plants and their inhuman time, plants that want to dispense with all other plants, the hypertrophied Gramineae intent on world domination; those are the truest beasts of the apocalypse, the biologist understands, some species of plants, the national-socialist pasture, the sugarcane of the enslaved, who have run out of time, the plane tree no more than a magnified blade of grass, the oil palm; the pasture has been conspiring for millennia to take over, and we are tyrannized by it; those two men are two of the millions of robots programmed by corporations, pretending to act on behalf of capital when they're really at the disposal of the plants, the master plan of the plants at the end of all time. The day, since we've arrived at the very last day, falls quickly, plunges toward its last horizon, leaves without saying good-bye to the last men left. Night falls in the cane field. We're all at the mercy of plants, the biologist thinks, finally catching sight of the man in the blue suit, which silvers as he readies to set fire to the field in total darkness. We're going to burn it all, the Black man says, is programmed to say, We're going to burn it all so the cycle can start again, so nothing is left but sugarcane and more sugarcane, oh, that sugarcane's sweet, almost as sweet as life, a very good imitation of life, a convincing imitation. And the biologist quotes back some lyrics that come to mind, *No cane field ever rests, if it's lucky, if it's blessed, it will be aguardiente,* just as it's starting to burn again, and the fire shakes loose its twelve thousand petals, and anyone would think it was trying and failing to take flight, tied to the canes it's consuming, which won't let it go, which hold on tight to its legs, so all the air fills with that odor, sweet things that imitate life, and the biologist and the Black man look at each other, both of them malprogrammed robots, and think: Tomorrow the hacienda will be entirely covered in ash. As always and as ever, atop the unfazed surface, there will float a fine film of chaff: the primordial soup in which future life-forms rehearse.

14.

On Monday morning, driving to school, the biologist scanned the radio. He was sick of the news, and keeping one eye on the highway, he turned the knob clockwise, counterclockwise, but there was only grating music, Christian talk stations, and more news. He eventually switched off the radio and started to think about when he should give his notice. He felt guilty for not seeing his contract through, walking out on the director—the one person there for whom he felt any fondness. Finding a replacement won't be easy, he thought, they'll be upset. There was also still a chance the study would fall through. Better to be sure, he reasoned, before I announce anything.

The morning was cool but the sun was already sticking, strong on the faces of campesinos biking along the highway, past coffee fields, up the mountain.

He got there early and thought he might be the first, a thought he confirmed in the empty teachers' lounge. On his desk was an unexpected manila envelope, his name scrawled across it in old-fashioned, bowlegged penmanship, as if someone ancient had written it. He tore it open without thinking, and inside, in a bundle of

aromatics—rosemary, basil, culantro, mint—was a note
from his uncle, mailed from the group home. The biologist could barely decipher the writing; the letters had
stuck, had caramelized, which made and unmade meaning and fractured each word at its core:

Dwarfopolis, Aprilor Mayor Jun e,

    Therewasoncea goodbrother andab adbrother.
And in betweenoneandtheother wasw here the
piggy's t ail twisted.
    You are the goodbrother piggy or y our the bad
brot hert wistedt ail.
    A work able brother or stiff. ¿? ¿? All creaturesa
regod's.
    Satan$$$$pastor took brother. They too kbrother
to the mount$$$$ainTossed him in the river. That's
why they never found him%%%%. Come seeme, I have
something f or you&&&&.
    Your unc&le.

He put all of it, note and herbs, back in the envelope.
Could he really be doing that badly? He tried calling the
home, but the number he found on the internet returned
only the usual sounds of misdirected communication:
electronic snarl, crossed wires, buzz. He tried again, dialed

several times, waited in vain to see if the noise would turn into a normal tone.

After a while, he went off to teach his first classes, guilty conscience swirling in his chest, and just like that, distracted, he started to talk about climate change in front of the obligatory hairstyles. But he didn't talk, he recited, like a preacher who had suddenly lost faith: Human activities are the root cause of almost all climate change, we might go so far as to think of ourselves as a geologic agent. We're destroying the planet, we're radically changing all life, but there's no turning back, it's too late. What's on the surface isn't enough for us, we're even worse than the weevils, we scour the depths of the earth to extract gold, coal, and petroleum. We're a blight. The ice caps are melting. Year after year, the sea level rises. Extreme weather: droughts and floods.

The students had heard about all this before, in many other contexts, and they didn't seem impressed by his apocalyptic tale.

The girl with the tip of a belly raised her hand. Can I go to the bathroom? she asked.

The teacher said no, she'd have to wait until break, and went on with his lesson.

A few minutes later, the girl raised her hand again. Can I go to the bathroom, please, teacher? It's an emergency, she insisted, I can't wait till break.

There was a murmur of protest in the classroom, but the teacher wasn't going to give them his arm to twist. The girls had been taking advantage of his patience; he was better off acting inflexible so they would learn.

The biologist went on about climate catastrophe, facing the large window to avoid additional interruption. For several minutes, he intoned: Scientists warn that the atmosphere is steadily losing oxygen, scientists warn that pandemics will become frequent, diseases and famines will surge.

When he turned to make sure everything was in order, he saw the same hand was raised.

Teacher, I really need to go the bathroom, repeated the girl with the tip of a belly.

Only then did the biologist notice the face below the obligatory hairstyle: tears, an expression of animal desperation.

Startled, he stepped toward her to get a better look and realized that the girl's water had already broken. Her legs were soaked. Not wasting a second, he called for an ambulance and sent another student for the director. He felt the pregnant girl's belly to measure the frequency of the contractions. It was all very alarming. The classroom was in turmoil. The other girls were completely out of control.

Teachers in nearby rooms heard the commotion and came over. Soon there was a group of them ringing the scene. Only the young math teacher offered to help, but she saw the amniotic fluid splattered on the ground and the girl's legs and started gagging. She almost vomited, her eyes watered. Easy, the biologist said, easy. If you want to help, why don't you try calling for an ambulance again. We need an ambulance, now.

The director pushed through the students and teachers, took one look at the biologist's face, and realized the situation was grave. It'll be half an hour before they get here, she said, decisive as always. We'll have to take her ourselves.

The fat PE teacher and a scrawny guy who taught philosophy improvised a stretcher with a sheet and carried the girl out to the biologist's Mazda, all under the supervision of the director, who climbed into the back seat next to her. Drive carefully, OK? she said to the biologist.

They started down the rural highway and hadn't gone even three miles when the pregnant girl let out a furious shriek. The director tried to calm her. But the girl continued to scream. She was screaming like an animal, and the scream crossed through the other passengers' bodies like a warning, its ancient origins in the depths of the limbic brain, the prehistoric brain, and the biologist and the director both felt their hair stand on end.

The girl lay down as much as the back seat allowed, forcing the director into one corner. The animal howling continued. The pregnant body writhed like a giant larva.

Go faster! the director shouted. Go as fast as you can!

The biologist obeyed. Doing his best to avoid the patches of unpaved road, forcing the Mazda's old engine to its maximum, he reached the main highway.

Between screams, the young woman tore off her skirt, her underwear, preparing for the next phase of her transformation.

The director noted that her vagina was very dilated, it was fully open and fleshy, as if it were flowering, wet, throbbing: each grimace on the director's face drew a response, the revelation of new petals, new folds, new slimy tongues, and that second face showed an expressive range much greater than the screams of the woman above, on the other end of the larva.

The director knew the vagina was capable of recreating expressions in a way that went far beyond mimesis, far beyond simple imitation. It wasn't copying but translating—everything remade in its own code. The opening widened and widened, so much so that something hairy began to push out from inside.

We're too late, the director said, knowing she'd been out-expressioned. Stop here. We'll just have to do what we can.

They pulled over next to a stall selling freshly baked pandebono and cold koumiss. The biologist hurried to take charge.

The elderly couple running the pandebono stall soon figured out what was happening and brought over a bucket of water, a towel, toilet paper, and scissors, which the biologist tried to sterilize with alcohol.

The vagina looked every one of them in the eye and went on opening; the girl screamed. The hairy thing kept pressing out.

The head emerged: a single slug of long, limp black hair.

The rest of the baby looked normal. A normal baby.

The biologist tugged on its little body until it was all the way out. He cut the cord with the scissors. The placenta dropped onto the cheap upholstery like an extraterrestrial substance.

The two from the pandebono stand got on their knees and prayed, eyes so inclined toward the sky that they went entirely white.

The director covered her face with both hands and shook her head, refusing, refusing.

The biologist held the baby up by its ankles and gave it a gentle pat so it would cry. And it cried.

Its cry was also normal. It was a baby, its face was just covered in hair.

The biologist, examining further, noticed a cluster of small and possibly permanent protrusions, chitinous in look and feel, on the posterior of the head. They were all a very intense shade of black, like dark fingernails or raised scales.

After wrapping the newborn up in the towel, the biologist handed him to the mother, who was no longer howling and even smiled. He looks healthy, the obstetrician said, though he has some hair on his face, and a couple of bumps on the back of his head.

The girl didn't stop smiling: entirely mother's love.

When they had all calmed down a little, when the director had finally pulled her hands from her face, the biologist announced that it was time, now, to take the mother and her little one to the clinic.

Before saying good-bye, the elderly couple from the pandebono stand gave the baby a prayer card of Jude the Apostle, patron saint of lost causes.

The newborn had stopped crying and slept on his mother's chest as the Mazda approached the limits of the dwarf city. The director was in the passenger seat, face rigid, as if robbed of all emotion, and the biologist tried to comfort her, placing a hand on her shoulder. You OK? he asked. The director tried but failed to contrive a smile.

The girl stared out the window then, anguish on her face. Don't take me to that clinic. Please, she dared to say. Not that one. The biologist looked in the rearview mirror. The director covered her face with both hands again. The biologist asked why not, if it was something to do with her health plan. The young woman didn't answer right away. She looked around first, in every direction, as if to make sure they weren't being followed. If we go there, she said, if we go to that clinic, they'll take my baby away.

The biologist smiled paternally, assuring her that no one would take her baby, not there and not anywhere else. Do you want us to call the father? he asked. Give me his number, I'll do it right now.

Through the rearview mirror, the young woman returned his smile with such defiance it left him cold. My baby doesn't have just one dad, she said. He has lots of them. But only one is his true father: the Knight of Faith.

The director, who'd been silent all that time, face hidden in her hands, came out from her well of denial. It makes no difference, she said to the girl, they're going to find you. It doesn't matter where you hide.

15.

Only one of you at a time, barked the guard at the entrance to the Faithful Servants emergency room. The director seized her chance to say good-bye. I have to get back to school, she said, you go in with her. And she hurried out, head down, like she didn't want to be seen there.

The biologist was alone with the girl and the baby covered in hair. A kind young doctor applauded his composure. Who knows what would have happened if you hadn't been there, he said. Are you in medicine? No, the biologist replied, I'm a biologist, but I've seen a few animal births—cows, horses. A veterinarian? asked the doctor. No, no, I'm not a veterinarian, said the biologist, I'm just familiar with the procedure.

All right, I guess that makes you quite a father, then, said the doctor, eyes bloodshot, mouth pasty, lines of thick saliva at the corners of his lips. His hair was dirty and unkempt. The biologist thought he probably had some disorder, or some addiction, or both. I sure would have liked to have a dad like you, said the doctor, mostly to himself. The biologist knew the working conditions at clinics like these were degrading, low pay and hellish shifts, and it wasn't uncommon for staff to end up with drug dependencies. I'm not the father, explained the biologist. I'm just her teacher. The doctor looked at him, squinting a little, and said that student-teacher attraction wasn't the strangest thing in the world, but he'd need to wait outside until they finished the exams. We'll be putting the baby in an incubator, he said, as if in trance. He's a little premature, so he's underweight. And of course, we'll do a few tests, standard procedure. He's a beautiful, healthy baby, but he has his little things, just like any newborn.

In the waiting room, the biologist sat with a crowd of women from the dwarf city's poorest neighborhoods, all of whom looked like they'd spent the night right there. They seemed resigned to the Byzantine system, identically dazed. There was a TV with the volume so low that it was both irritating and soothing.

The biologist disliked conspiracy theories. He had always found them inelegant, heavy-handed, and bound to favor simple and ideological explanations for complex phenomena, often relying on fallacies, circular logic, implausible correlations, and argumentative ambushes. On the other hand, conspiracy did offer schemas of understanding in contexts where absurdity threatened to obscure everything, or so the biologist thought. There, where the risk of collective delirium is at its highest, where the cultivation of reason and logic is scorned, five-cent explanations sell like hotcakes, placebos for consciousness, substitutes for rationality, which makes it easier to just shroud any phenomenon in mystery, perpetuate slowness and backwardness: then any event is material for fiction. And fiction with no respect for the primacy of facts is fundamentally anti-scientific. That's what he was thinking about in the waiting room, surrounded by women whose cerebrums the TV had been sopping up since the night before. But even as a skeptic, the biologist couldn't shake the uncomfortable feeling that the whole world was in on something, and he was the only person naive enough to pass through it and never figure out what.

That's when the doctor came in and told him they'd done an emergency transfer, mom and baby were on their way to another clinic, but not to worry, the girl's prepaid health plan will cover it all.

Anyway, said the doctor, a little distraught, you're not the father, right? Just the teacher. Well, rest assured that your student is in good hands.

The biologist finally understood that, if he was before some cabal, if what his senses were being offered in those moments was representation, a smoke screen, the whole thing couldn't be clumsier, not with that stick figure playing a role. Did they think he was stupid?

He had to try hard not to hit the doctor, grab his shoulders and shake him. If I hit him, he thought, they'll think I'm the crazy one. And that's when he realized he was already adrift in the logic of a conspiracy, and had been for who knows how long.

16.

He left the clinic, almost crawling from the shock of intellectual defeat. There was nothing to do but start walking.

Absorbed by a music of thousands of crossed wires, which only he could hear, he left that grim tract of hospitals, pharmacies, funeral homes. The little will he had left he bestowed on an empty street that led him past the ruins of the old zoo—small and modest, like everything in the dwarf city. It now consisted only of empty cages, tall grass, a few guava trees.

Later he crossed a small bridge and arrived at the crumbling university sports complex. He stood there for a while, looking through the fence: diving platforms, drained pools, empty soccer fields. In the distance, a few runners circled the track. The landscape's outmoded Cartesianism, barely disturbed by his human presence, layered the music that buzzed in his head with a faint artificial harmony. He released a long sigh and for several minutes gave in, narcotized by the emaciated geometry: the lines and semicircles; the warped wooden backboards with rusted hoops; the huge rectangle of the field, perfect, white, and symmetrical; the soft ellipses that suggested discernible, quantifiable paths. It's obvious that something very complex is happening here, he thought, but it's too early to hypothesize—I need data. He was sure about one thing, though: he was leaving his job at the school. I don't think I'll ever go back, he thought before walking on. I won't even ask for my last paycheck.

Then he wandered through other parts of the campus, past the rationalist structures of the school of engineering and, a little farther on, the hill where they'd put student housing.

He sat down on a concrete bench right at the foot of some rosemary, in the untended garden delimiting two sets of buildings. The scent made him think of the note his uncle had written him, the envelope full of herbs. It was something about his brother. Or that's what he'd deciphered in the trampling of letters. His brother. His brother. My brother.

The biologist was aware that he had spent years constructing a barrier to hold back all thoughts of his brother, his brother's death. I guess I'll never be a true Humboldtian, he thought, smiling sadly. A true Humboldtian wouldn't just map out paranoid tangles of facts; he'd also try to establish profound connections. Or rather, a true Humboldtian would understand that the whole network of seemingly automatic inter-organism relations can only truly be understood if you acknowledge the role of emotion. *Naturgemälde,* the nature painting—he never could have done it without accepting his singularity, the fine and tenuous space from which he was looking, listening, speaking. Only then could he render the world as image: fragmentary, segmented, not at all dominant or imperious; the opposite, in fact. A humble yet colorful miniature of the universe.

The biologist remembered his first introduction to that idea, as a kid on his uncle's plot, where he and his brother used to go to observe the hummingbirds. If you're Américan, you're a naturalist, and vice versa, their uncle would say, and sometimes, very rarely, delivering this motto would put him in a mood, and he'd be suddenly holding forth, almost maniacal: Américan, revolutionary, naturalist—it's all the same, all of it! They're synonyms, he would say, just look at the bills the central bank's spitting out. What do you see on almost every one of them? On the front, there's a founding father, a revolutionary, a guerrilla of the Republic, and on the back, there's some kind of plant or animal, or some monumental geographic accident. Revolution is what started our clock ticking. It hasn't stopped since. And the clock of revolution is nature's clock made manifest. Sure, there might be days when it seems like that can't be true, maybe you'll think the revolution is over, the counterforces won out, but don't let them fool you, oh no. Revolution's life itself, it's nothing more or less, and life is an irreversible force, unleashed millions of years ago. Sometimes you think death might conquer life, but I'm telling you, it doesn't: life outwits death every time, just open your billfold, it's there, clear as any landscape, he'd say. And the humming-birds danced in unison, and they listened like children fascinated and mystified by the circus. The division of labor was more than clear to their uncle: the biologist would be a man of science, fluent in categories and measurements, a diligent taxonomist who studied the Andean short-faced bear, his favorite of the animals native to the region; whereas his brother, more sensitive, more gentle, would play the role of artist. And that's how it was for years, until his brother, influenced by a mother with other plans for the light of her life, began to disdain not only his role in the equation but also their uncle's many aesthetic delusions. After a certain point in early adolescence, the biologist's brother rolled his eyes at every one of the old man's screeds and on a few occasions even dared talk back. He would repeat what he'd overheard, mention the uncle's stint in jail, the way it must have affected him. A few years after that, eager to fulfill the maternal mandate, the brother became a regular at the gym, destroyed all evidence of his queerness, and announced that he'd study law and pursue a career in politics. Of course he never returned to his uncle's plot to observe the hummingbirds. Only fags waste their time watching birds, he would say.

The biologist, who couldn't renounce his naturalist calling but didn't want to make enemies of his mother and his brother, opted for a moderate position, far from his uncle's fervent political radicalism. After all, he thought, science is pure, it's superior. You can hold your head high as a naturalist and leave out the Américan part, the revolutionary part. I just want to study animals, he repeated again and again, to convince himself that his science was autonomous, his character moderate; and if that helps me get out of this sorry excuse for a city, even better.

There on the concrete bench, swathed in the scent of rosemary, the biologist could finally see it all seething in the same drawing: feelings, ideas, data; his memories of his uncle; a baby whose face was covered in hair; a prosthetic leg; a virgin standing alone in a shell-shaped niche; his brother's murder; a man with the head of a beetle; a monocrop of buildings; the passionflower; Uncle Remus's bulging eyes; all of it lost in the zip-a-dee-doo-dah of time. He still didn't understand it, but at least the living image was taking shape. Maybe, thought the biologist, maybe it's time to go over to the old house.

17.

The old fuck who took care of the house for them answered the door, could hardly place the biologist, and almost turned him away. Ah, I remember you now, he said, but he continued to act put out. The biologist found this treatment outrageous—in his own home, in the house where he'd spent his childhood—but he was there for other reasons and kept quiet.

Everything inside was more or less the same apart from his room, which they'd set up for the bastard caretaker's junkie son. It seemed that, by order of his mother, all the biologist's things were now being stored in the basement. That didn't bother him much. It'd been years since he'd even dreamed of having a home on this side of the world; losing the bedroom seemed minor.

For a while he just walked around the house, went in and out of rooms under the strict surveillance of the old fuck. What can I do for you, young man? the meddler asked unfeelingly. How can we be of service? Whatever you need. And similar formulations. The biologist didn't once answer; the puckering asshole eventually gave up and left him alone. Anyway, he wasn't sure what he was looking for. At first he'd just wanted to see the old house, step back inside after all those years, confirm it was still standing. Not even the ancient toad could sour that experience for him.

From the odor that rushed out when he opened some of the doors, the biologist knew there were rooms no one had entered for years. He ran his hand over the furniture, a ghost who wanted to coat himself in that dust, in the aroma of something kept, and even peered into the flowerpots in search of his uncle's keys, but all he found were his mother's cigarette butts—good fertilizer, supposedly. The biologist was delighted by even that detail, filled with gratitude for his mother, who had no reason to keep that house, much less pay for a caretaker. The doddering shithead seemed like a lesser evil when he thought about the advantages of maintaining the family home.

After several rounds, he made up his mind to enter his brother's room, which was still suffused with the same cologne. A fragrance for men, made to cover up all other odors. A smothering layer of virile power and seemliness that hung in the air ten years later.

The biologist rifled through drawers, examined papers, paged through sterile law and statistics textbooks, photo albums, looked in the closet, scanned shirts and suits, and suddenly realized all that was there was his brother's thick scab of officialdom. Not one possession gave him away: no porn stashed under the mattress, not a single compromising object. Not even in the trash on his computer, a machine still running Windows 95, where everything was sorted into folders for work, and correspondence, and sales-and-purchase agreements. His brother had been assiduous in holding his sexuality at arm's length, far from his public life as a lawyer, real estate agent, and, near the end, authority on rural property law.

The biologist tried to remember the moment the change was effected, from sweet kid to ruthless executive, always arrogant, on the defensive, what circumstances had triggered it. Ideally he would have found something, a clue or a letter, maybe—a letter addressed to him, in its own folder on the computer—and there, his brother would reveal everything, finally shedding light on the cause of his death. Dear brother, there's something I want to tell you, a secret that, for years, has been eating away at me . . . But that was asking too much, the biologist knew it. His brother believed accounts could only be rendered in spreadsheets; the biologist had plenty of proof of that. Someone more methodical would comb through every file, try to read between the lines. *Follow the money,* that's what they say in detective novels, he thought. Knowing he wasn't that person, he skimmed several spreadsheets and only discerned projections and speculations, illusions of deals. He was relieved not to find any transfers of large sums of cash, nor any sign of significant debt. The spreadsheets painted a clear picture: he was a serious, accommodating man who had every chance of success, who kept everything in its place, whose virtues their mother trumpeted—what a catch, he even joined the country club, the perfect date for an evening at the bullring.

One night a decade earlier, the biologist left the lab, where he'd been analyzing urine samples from brown bears, and got a transatlantic phone call from their mother. They'd found his brother's body in a ditch, he'd been shot eight times in the head. The biologist got on a plane and was back in the dwarf city two days later, supporting his mother through the arrangements and public investigation. The biologist's memories of those days were hazy. The grief and rage intermixed, and later, the feeling of absolute powerlessness—the public attorney was slow, and his findings were dubious. At first, mostly thanks to the work of a local reporter from *El Liberal,* the investigation centered on a land dispute between some palm-oil executives and a Black farmer collective on the Pacific coast. According to the reporter, his brother had been against an attempt to formalize the transfer of illicitly usurped lands, which must have led to his murder. Under the pressure of media frenzy, the prosecutors could only follow the lead, and early on, the case file grew thick with reports on that scheme and others the same business had carried out. That's how, digging, digging, they started to chance upon the traces, inevitable slips, and finally, witnesses who would come to reveal his brother's secret life: local clubs, online profiles, emails, sexts, even a few pictures in which he'd posed in a feather headdress and nothing else. These unexpected findings transformed their approach to the case, and within days, another theory gained traction: it was a crime of passion between homosexuals, which attracted much more media attention, although the reporter at *El Liberal* was still insisting on litigation gone bad. Their mother was indignant, and in vain she seized upon all her political friendships, hoping to keep the story from getting out. For a couple of days, on the radio, on local TV, in the op-eds, they talked of nothing but gay murderers, toxic love affairs, perversions they called unspeakable. The prosecution, however, took no position. And a few weeks after that, around the time when everyone else had forgotten about the case, three culprits turned up; the police ID'd them as members of a kidnapping ring who'd sold hostages to several armed communist groups. In exchange for a reduced sentence, said the chief of police on the radio, with the characteristic diction of local law enforcement, the criminals confessed to the kidnapping and subsequent murder of the biologist's brother. Once the terrorist front had acquired their victim, they planned to extort money from the family, which we know to be common practice among these radicals, he explained. But we have reason to believe the deal went bad, and now the authorities need to figure out why.

The prosecutors hurried to endorse the chief's hypothesis, and all parties involved seemed satisfied. Even their mother stopped asking questions about the ordeal and focused on the spiritual work of grieving. But still, the case was never closed: there was no conclusive evidence aside from the alleged perpetrators' testimonies, and the stubborn reporter at *El Liberal* carried on with his lonely plight for some time.

Months went by, and the three convicts died in prison. They didn't kill them all at once, there were weeks between the deaths, and they never repeated a circumstance or a method. Suffocation, poison, stabbing. Those cases were never closed either. Everything hung in suspense, on the perpetual verge of paralysis, the flow of a river of wet cement hardening swiftly underneath the tropical sun.

The reporter from *El Liberal* wrote one last piece about his brother's case, concluding, with the characteristic diction of local journalists: There's no better way to kill a story than by making it more and more convoluted, drowning it in useless and upsetting information. The reader's attention disperses across its thousand and one branches. The plot holds neither water nor attention. And that's it, ladies and gentlemen, that's how they do it. That's how the snakes and swindlers craft this nation's impunities.

After they published that piece, the reporter received death threats and moved to another city, where he could no longer do his job. He started selling appliances near the Ecuadorian border and did all he could to distance himself from journalism.

Their mother hadn't liked that last article either. Amid her anguish, amid her weeping, the black veils and the endless phone calls with consolatrices, she found solace in the fact that her son's good name, his heterosexuality, had been recovered. And she was well aware of the chasm between a queer lovers' quarrel and Marxist terrorism as far as reputation was concerned—in other words, Mother knew how to leverage a tragedy. With the perspective distance had granted him, with detached scientific interest, the biologist quickly confirmed that the specter of armed groups had granted their house an air of gentility: they were now and forevermore on the side of decent people, fair and just, almost majestic in their suffering. And as his own mother proved in the years that followed, a little aptitude and some contacts were all it took to exploit the situation and gain access to certain heavyweights, reap the spoils and largesse of the highest tier. He just had to play the game well, and his mother was the best player, cunning, masterful.

The biologist never discounted any of the hypotheses, mostly because not one of them conjured the brother he knew: not the lover who could unleash wild passion in others, nor the man of principle willing to challenge executives, surely acquaintances of his, for no reason except to defend the rights of a cheated minority, and while anyone not looking closely enough might have taken his brother for a young millionaire, the twists and inconsistencies in the police account undermined the version involving kidnapping and extortion. Ultimately, that tangle of fabrications had only further distorted his image of his brother. Who was he really? Had he known his brother at all? Or to be more precise, which brother was the truest one? The sensitive child who liked to make art, or the suit drenched in cologne, refusing to come out of the closet even when so many people who shared his background, social and educational, were starting to do just that? Were the two versions really so different? He wondered if they were communicating vessels of some kind; at least that would give them some unity and coherence. Or maybe a complete organism, able to hold contradictions between parts and functions.

With so much time having passed, the biologist concluded that it no longer made sense to obsess over truth, much less justice. Now it was a matter of deciding, and he had no doubt about which brother he preferred. The tenderhearted queer, that's my brother, the skillful birdwatcher, the fabulist who invented us imaginary fathers, thought the biologist, for me, at least, that's my brother, my playmate and accomplice, the kid who once had me convinced that our dad—our real dad, not the one from the previous year who'd turned out to be a fake, no, this was our actual father—worked in the circus, doing motorcycle stunts inside a giant metal sphere . . . Those enormous steel globes with motorcyclists inside, are they still around? Is there some circus where you can find one? the biologist digressed, scanning useless papers in his brother's room. Do circuses still exist? A while ago, they'd put a megamart in the lot where the traveling circus used to make camp. It's possible they still come, that they've just been cast out to some other less visible place. The biologist, deep in the memory, saw himself with his brother, going to shows five, six, seven days in a row just to see their fictitious father, their true father. We finally found him, his brother leaned over to whisper. Then the lights went out all at once, the crowd became a broth of shining eyes, and a voice said, Now for the most daring feat of all, and almost instantly, they assembled the giant steel sphere in the shadows. They heard the first notes of "The Final Countdown," a fanfare that sent an electric jolt up the kids' spines, and with all the theatrical pomp you could imagine, two motorcyclists appeared, one dressed in black and the other—the one who his brother insisted was their father—in white. He's that one, just look at him, the one in white, he said. He walks just like us, it's Him. The music got quiet, and the two motorcyclists, in ceremonial total silence, entered the sphere, and there, they wove a duel of roaring pirouettes, a new music of motors and smoke and metallic rumbles. At the end of every show, the two boys would wait in an interminable line then pay twenty pesos to take a polaroid with the motorcyclists, who never—not once—took their helmets off. This time we're going to talk to him, said his brother. We'll say, Dad, it's us, your kids, will you take us out on your bike? But they never did. They waited almost half an hour in line, dying of nerves, anxious to see their father, and when they got to the front, they just paid, tense and not saying a word; they took a photo with their arms around the man in the white suit and left. Tomorrow we'll come back. Tomorrow we'll really say something, they swore on the way home, happy. And his brother, methodical in his lies, disciplined, learning how to pluck the hidden strings of simulation, would hold up the polaroid and say, Did you notice he has our eyes? Tomorrow we'll ask him to take us out on his bike, show us how to do tricks like he does, and when we're big, we'll have our own bikes and our own really cool suits, mine'll be neon pink and shiny in the dark, and yours'll be white, just like Dad's, white with gold stripes.

18.

That night, he met the dealer in the plaza, partly because he was out of drugs and partly because he needed to talk to a friend. They sat in the same place as always, on a bench in the middle of the park, in front of a modest statue, almost obscured by the trees. The biologist liked the blend of scents in the air: marijuana smoke, the nocturnal freshness of plants. Relaxed, he attempted a summary of everything he had been through the last few days. It all started when we were out drinking the other night, he said. Complete chaos. The dealer was most interested in his brother, asked several questions about the case, and concluded that they'd never have an answer, since there was no way of gathering new information, but so it goes. So it goes in this dust cloud. The dealer smoked without stopping, words pouring out of him. You don't even know where to start when you're telling a story, because there isn't really a story, there's just misdirection. Haven't you noticed? It was the same with my dad and my granddad. They were just dead, we never knew why, and now it's better we don't, what for, and what's left is a pile of scraps, bits and bobs of stories, the worst story you ever heard, a mess of a story. It's just a bunch of beginnings that add up to nothing—like an art-house film, right? Like those movies the college kids like, in a language you never heard of . . . Pure chimbiadera, bróster, a fucking tease, that scene's barely getting the words out, and all in black and white, yeah, high art they call it, but what are you left with, besides that it puts you to sleep. I mean, for fuck's sake, I want my money back. The biologist said that's exactly how the reporter felt, the one from *El Liberal*. Which is to say, make a story complex enough and no one will want to hear it, much less retell it. And if no one retells a story, it's forgotten. It dies without having begun. Or maybe that's not true, maybe confusion gets passed along, the knot, from one mouth to the next. Inconclusive stories proliferate too, just like debts, the biologist said, also quite stoned. The dealer blew a chain of little smoke rings. A fucking tease, he said, try and untangle it, you'll go crazy. Better to leave it alone, parcero, and if you really want my advice? Start showering in the dark. That's the best way to get your head on straight. Trust me. Total darkness, the water nice and hot at first, you ease your way in, then cold, freezing. Then hot again, and so on. I swear to you, every so often, I'm showering, and it hits me: so many things are happening just in my head, how do I put this—I see how most of the stuff I think of as real is basically my own production.

Things my head put together itself, without my permission. And right there, in the shower, the darkness and all that good water around me, I see, I can really see: goddamn, it's all clear all the sudden: half of anyone's life only exists in their head. And what's left after that, half of it happens in language, in fucking chatter, in noise, am I right? Only a quarter is real. I'm serious, parce, this is what's going to cure you. Just hear me out. Try it one day and you'll see—what you're telling me now, part of it, let's say a third, two-fourths, three-eighths, is happening only inside you or inside your language. Try it, just try it, you'll see.

A vibrating phone interrupted them. The director, calling to tell the biologist that she urgently needed to talk to him, she'd like him to come by her office first thing in the morning. I don't think I'll be coming back in, the biologist said, I'm giving my notice. What I mean to say is, I quit. The dealer turned sharply because he could hear the director shouting from inside the phone; the biologist waited out the performance. No, I won't be coming back to the school, he said, very certain now, once the woman allowed him to speak. Not tomorrow morning, not ever again, I want nothing to do with the place. The director let out a sigh and said once more that she needed to meet with him. It's urgent, she repeated, there are things we need to discuss. The biologist wanted to know if they couldn't discuss them by phone or email. No, that wasn't possible, it had to be in person. In the end, they agreed to meet the next day at one of the Archdiocese buildings. Why there? the biologist asked. It's better that way, the director said, no one's ever around. They hung up.

She's out for blood, isn't she, said the dealer. I heard the whole thing. The biologist laughed then coughed, his eyes increasingly swollen, although in his head, he was still weaving, weaving, connecting bits of ideas, images, memories, all in pursuit of the whole.

Tell me one thing, the biologist said, before I forget, because pretty soon I'll be wrecked, this is good stuff . . . but tell me one thing: Have you heard of the Knight of Faith?

The dealer looked at him sideways, blowing out off-yellow smoke. The Knight of Faith? he said. Sure, I've heard of it, couldn't miss it. That's my mom's church. A church? Yeah, for the true believers, with a parking lot for UFOs and everything. You know, one of those get-rich-quick setups Christians somehow rationalize to themselves. I tell my mom not to trust them, they're screwing her over—for fuck's sake, they never stop asking for money—but no power on Earth could bring her around. My old lady is very devoted. She prays all day long, parcero. She's bound hand and foot.

19.

The next morning he ate breakfast with his mother, who'd gotten up early to make the most of the day, or so she said when she sat down at the table. In the space around the two diners, the Indigenous woman fried eggs, heated arepas, brewed coffee, never saying a word, and she placed it all on the table with a repertoire of gestures developed over centuries to go unnoticed by the patroness and her son. It was the mother who broke the silence. I heard you went by the old house, she said. Did you need something? The biologist didn't look up from his plate and kept chewing. I went because I felt like it, Mom, it's my house. The rehydrated corpse informed you, I take it? The mother was well aware that her son made comments like that to provoke her; she'd learned to ignore them.

Yesterday, at the store, the lady of the house went on after another silence, I ran into that girl you used to go out with. This time the biologist looked up. Who? he asked. Your girlfriend from a million years ago, the one who had the problem with her leg. Ah, her, the biologist said, feigning indifference, though he knew already that his mother had him spinning in her palm. She said they want you for that study, with the weevils. Are you going to say yes? The biologist told her he needed to give it some thought. I'm not sure yet, I haven't seen a contract. And the thought of working in palm oil doesn't exactly thrill me. It's no secret how that industry took off. Look it up, you'll see. Stolen land, ruthless deforestation, dead all over the country. And another thing: those palms turn farmable land into desert, they'll destroy whatever ecosystem you put them in, just like any monocrop—the soil is useless for decades. It's a plague, a plague that sets off other plagues, or maybe a plague within a plague within a plague. Then there's the ecological footprint, waste management, let's just say the palm's no friend to nature. Like I said, I'm considering it. The work itself is interesting, it's all about biochemistry and pheromones, but I haven't decided yet.

His mother listened and said nothing, stabbing his face with her eyes, forcing the biologist to look away several times.

That poor little thing, the mother said. I haven't seen her since you were kids. She's darling, sweet as ever, so polite, so charming. Such a shame about her leg, isn't it? . . . She said you went down to your brother's old girlfriend's place. All the old flames in one room, huh? Isn't that house incredible? Just gorgeous.

The biologist went along with it all by lowing intermittently.

And how about that telenovela, the mother continued, now on a roll. What an idea, a telenovela set on an old hacienda. What vision. Did they tell you when it'll be out? No, the biologist knew nothing, and he was looking at his mother now, his eyes now wide and frenzied, and he thought, Shipwrecked by history, and his mother looked back with a mother's eyes. With mammal eyes and mammal love and a mammal's death drive and tenderness. And the biologist felt guilt and fear and also disgust, and gratitude too, love and respect, because he knew that his mammal had sacrificed everything for her children, had relinquished herself to push forward her brood—bachelors, queers, slackers, and madmen.

20.

He stood in front of the entrance to the Archdiocese museum and looked up and down the street in case the director was there, but he saw only a line of cars; the high wall of the church of Santo Domingo, dirty white like a page from a schoolkid's notebook; and people drift-ing around the small plaza in front of the law building, some on their way into or out of the corner café, others street vendors slipping between cars. To the biologist, all this seemed normal and predictable, like anything nature repeated with mechanical regularity. A sunny afternoon in the historic center of the dwarf city.

Behind a table in the entrance hall was an old woman with the face of a sea turtle, in short sleeves that revealed her impressively wrinkled arms. The biolo-gist wasn't sure what to do. He approached the table and asked if she'd seen a woman about this tall, with dark hair and very big eyes. The turtle looked at him, impassive, and, with the slowness inherent to her spe-cies, turned her head toward the exhibition entrance, next to which was an attendant in the classic maroon uniform. Neither of the two had seen a woman of that description. Hardly anyone comes here, she said. We'd remember.

The biologist called the director but couldn't get through. He texted her: I'm here. She responded a few seconds later: Give me five minutes, I'll meet you inside.

He paid for a ticket, and the turtle, having informed him that they were out of brochures, passed him a scrap of red paper that he then handed to the attendant in what seemed to the biologist a strange procedure given the proximity of the two parties. If each of them, old woman and attendant, had reached toward the other instead, they'd have achieved the same result. A transaction in which I'm entirely expendable, he thought.

The biologist hadn't been there since the compulsory high-school visit twenty, twenty-five years ago. It was a modest but respectable museum; some of the religious art was quite valuable. The discreet wall text, designed not to detract too much from the gravitas of the structure, explained that the dwarf city had initially been a mere consumer of artwork from Europe or Quito but then, during a brief period of splendor between the seventeenth and eighteenth centuries, became a small hub for the production of religious images, with its own workshops for painting, sculpture, and gold- and silversmithing. The prized items in the collection were without a doubt the custodiae, those spectacular apparatuses dripping gold and gemstones whose function in the liturgy the biologist had never understood. Standing in front of the display cases, all of them lit up theatrically, he recalled his childhood awe during each formidable Holy Week mass. What were the custodiae, exactly? What class of magical amulet? Were they vessels, hypertrophied chalices that could no longer hold any liquid? Or were they more like lamps that lit the path to salvation? Or maybe they were swords deformed and made blunt by ornamental excess? Doubtless they'd been endowed with special powers, like antennae that received divine signals then decoded them for the eyes of the parishioners, into the universal language of merchandise. Following the wall text, the biologist observed that, as with the most extravagant paintings, the fabrication of custodiae had flourished during the Counter-Reformation, when the Catholic Church set in motion its major propaganda operation: the colonization of the senses through artwork. Persuasion wasn't enough anymore, subjugation was the aim. The passage from education to spectacle, evangelization to fanaticism. These images were made to trap the eye and flood it with vibration, illusions of movement, space-time dislocation.

Overwhelmed by the special effects, the biologist paused in front of a painting true to the usual standards for portraying a virtuous scene. A classic decorative

pattern with vegetal motifs filled the better part of the
canvas—berries, vines, a few passionflowers with big,
meaty petals—and at the center, framed within a key-
hole, small compared to the space that surrounded her,
was the image of martyr Saint Barbara: a woman on her
knees, an executioner raising his sword, on the verge of
beheading her. In the background, a few forks of red
lightning fell upon a domed tower. It was as if the spec-
tator were sneaking looks at the scene, peering into a
trunk through its lock. Or maybe it was the opposite:
maybe the painter meant to suggest that the viewer was
inside the trunk and could, from there, bear witness to the
crime. A curious comment on perspective: viewer captive
in a box, inside a camera obscura: a camera obscura—
the brain—inside a camera obscura—the trunk; the view-
ing angle constricted, but by whom? Who had dictated
the field of vision's arbitrary limits?

The biologist had never seen a religious painting
make use of that technique. He read the placard: "*The
Martyrdom of Saint Barbara*. Anonymous. Seventeenth
century. Oil on canvas. Altar frontispiece."

He was about to look up the martyrology of Saint
Barbara but saw that he had a message from the director, sent barely a minute earlier. Just getting here, it said,
wait for me in the courtyard. Dutiful, he went down to
the ground floor and began to pace from one side of the

courtyard to the other, gaze fixed on the stones under-
foot. He was there for several minutes, glancing at his
phone every so often, putting it back in his pocket, pulling it out to check the time. The director didn't show up.
He sent another message—I'm in the courtyard—and a
few minutes later, he saw it had been read.

He returned to the galleries, immersing himself again
in religious objects, which suddenly seemed as compelling
as plant or animal samples. He couldn't look away from
a pair of cherub sculptures he found extremely obscene.
Child pornography, he thought, letting out a snort that
was audible all across the room. The only other museum-
goer, an older man—maybe a white-collar worker retired
and taking his leisure, unshaven and poorly dressed—
turned to give him a look. The biologist raised one hand to
beg his pardon then went out to the courtyard to call the
director. He called twice, three times, four, and nothing. He sent another message: Are you coming? I'm still
here. Again, no response. Just two small blue checkmarks
showing the message had been delivered and read.

He kept circling the museum, passing by what he'd
already seen, although this time he paid more attention to some of the details. Tiny torture scenes, meteors,
miracles, in the backgrounds or far corners of the main
images, like commentaries or footnotes: a little man, face-
down and bowlegged, whom two sawyers were cutting

in half at the crotch; a flying Beatus; the still life fore-
shadowed at a last-supper table; and miniature animals
scattered across all the paintings: little lambs, pigs, mon-
keys, birds—and a butterfly, almost invisible, perched on
the veil of the Blessed Virgin. The word shot out of him
like an automatism: *imago*. Why do we call adult insects
imagoes? Who decided on that? Was it Linnaeus, who
left religious or moral traces in all he christened? *Imago*,
like the Latin word used to signify likeness, and the
name for the wax death masks made for senators and dis-
played at the Roman Forum. As if upon moving through
all the phases of metamorphosis, the insect was freed of
its mask, its true image was revealed: its authentic face,
the last rendering of its species. The last mask.

That's when the attendant came in to tell him that
the museum was closing soon, it was time to go. The
biologist followed him to the exit, and while they crossed
the cobbled courtyard, he checked his phone again, just
to make sure there was nothing from the director. At the
entrance hall, under the subtle scrutiny of the turtle and
the attendant, the biologist sent one more message: I'm
out of time. If there's something you want to tell me, you
can reach me here, or email me. Again: I'm leaving the
school. Send the girls my best.

Only then did the biologist realize that he was unem-
ployed again, with no prospects, one hand reaching back

and the other forward. Because frankly, he had serious doubts about the offer from his ex-girlfriend. Ethical doubts, technical doubts, suspicions about their seemingly chance encounter. That's paranoia, I know, he thought, but the doubts don't seem wholly unreasonable. They're based on facts, on hard data. Why solve the palm-weevil blight when the African palm is a blight in itself, and doubtless an even worse one? Sure, researching biochemical adaptations would help us better understand animal behavior in monocrops, and there'd be near-infinite applications for a serious study on pheromones, but that doesn't make up for the harm these palms inflict on their ecosystems. Palm monocropping causes desertification; over time, the land becomes sterile; the research confirms it. Period. I don't want any part in that, he thought as dusk came on and he gave himself up to wandering, avoiding the darkest streets. Despite everything, he felt relatively hopeful. Something would open up at the university, he was sure of it— patience. The slow tint of the evening light transformed the facades, orange to red, and next to the old mansions and churches, the roofs of the smallest houses seemed to bend in submission, allowing the sun to indulge them. In a fit of nostalgia, he stopped at a corner store that also sold baked goods, looked hard at the contents of all the glass cases, and decided on mantecadas that turned out to be tasteless and rubbery. They must have been the day-olds, and besides, they'd used wheat flour, not yuca—unforgiveable. He threw them out having barely tasted them. Those aren't mantecadas, they're doughnuts, he thought, to justify the waste but also make fun of himself for acting like an old man, a staunch defender of culinary tradition.

Meandering, he ended up in a neighborhood near the squat hills that bordered the eastern part of the city. Hardly anyone was around, and the silence heightened his loneliness. A few blocks on, the pedestrian came to the entrance of the pueblito, a small park where they'd built miniatures of the dwarf city's most recognizable buildings. The miniature of a miniature. The city applauding itself by way of diminutive replicas, raised a few blocks from originals. An eccentric mayor had thought of it twenty years earlier, and other illustrious citizens, fond of the city's beauty and magic, had eagerly backed him. Though they'd intended a solemn tribute to their great viceregal stronghold, the biologist found the pueblito kitschy at best, maybe pathetic. Wasn't it funny, even mysterious, that such an extravagant wish, such an earnest aspiration, found its end in the form of a miniature? Were all the major battles inscribed on grains of rice?

The biologist walked up and down the fake streets, delighting in the laughter the models drew from him, and thought of what he'd talked about with his childhood friend a while ago: the provincial sense of humor as a kind of determinist doctrine. An understated joke and also your sentence. Both aphorism and gag. A wisecrack expressed in a bolt of wit. A finely honed talent for nicknames.

He crossed a model of a famous bridge, left the pueblito, and went back to the silent streets, comforted, almost happy, what a nice walk, everything would be better soon, he was sure of it, that's how life is: average, with highs and lows. In the grips of that fit of optimism, he didn't hear the man who touched his back come up behind him. Nor did he know if he should have turned, since by then there was a second one coming from the front, with a pistol trained on his face. A four-by-four pickup with tinted windows stopped short beside the three of them. The rear door opened. The biologist had no time to react. They got him inside almost effortlessly, a succession of flawless and unfeeling movements carried out hundreds, thousands, of times.

In the truck, seeing that none of their faces were covered, the biologist understood there was no going back and that they would kill him.

All that was left to find out was when and how. And if he was lucky and had the chance, maybe he'd even learn why.

In a final useless gesture of desperation, he looked out the windows hoping for a miracle in the streets, a providential traffic jam, an accident, but one of the guys covered his head with a grocery bag, another took the cell phone from his pants pocket, the third bound his wrists with duct tape.

21.

When they pulled the sack from his head and freed his hands, it was night. The room was empty except for a mountain of bags of dog food and a shelf filled with large glass jars of transparent liquid. The biologist summoned all his deductive powers, tried to analyze and parse, but every explanation seemed insufficient, banal. My paranoia was justified, great, but this has to be a big misunderstanding, he thought, to calm himself down and keep from losing the little hope he had left. They have no reason to kill me.

On the upper part of one wall, he noticed a small window, just a hole, really, maybe too far off the ground. The biologist clambered onto the bags of dog food, jolted upward several times, and managed to see only the starry sky and the tops of some distant pines.

Two armed men entered the room, their faces also uncovered. The biologist's stomach burned, he felt acid consuming his throat, soon he would vomit.

They led him through a dimly lit warehouse in which he saw more shelves with the same glass jars and the same transparent liquid, only something seemed to be floating inside of these, something that, in the darkness, he couldn't discern. The biologist thought he saw movement. Were the things in those jars dead or living? He remembered what the dealer said he'd come to understand on his shower astral trips, the part about everything happening inside your head and inside your language: an excuse to forget your body, he thought, to remove it from the equation, even if just for a minute, but really, the body's the body. Everything that happens is the body. There is nothing outside of body. Or rather, what's outside the body happens within it. We're just like any other living organism. Now I'm going to die. They're going to tear the one thing I have away from me. I have nothing else. My defense mechanisms, what are they. Nervous sweating, an unpleasant smell. The biochemistry of fear.

Dogs were barking in the distance, but the clear sky over the pasture put a cool hush in the air. I won't ask to die quickly. I won't ask for anything. Won't even open my mouth. I won't give them the chance to improvise. They can do what they've planned and be done with it.

They stopped at a wooden door on the far end of the warehouse. One of the men went in. There were sounds of indistinct voices, and finally they summoned him into a room almost identical to the one with the dog food, except that here, beside the shelves of empty jars, there was a table covered in papers and cardboard file boxes, and a pair of wooden chairs with cowhide-upholstered backs. In one of the chairs was the man who looked newly retired, whom he'd seen loitering at the museum, now smiling with full and surprisingly feminine lips, and the biologist, alert to the sickly sweet sheen in his eyes, thought of two little windows beyond which there lay a cane plantation in flames and trembled with fear. He had to look away.

Sit down, comrade, sit down, the old man said, his tone playful, as if he were welcoming a close friend or a special guest. The biologist, not daring to meet his eyes again, stayed silent, livid, slicked with the sweat of panic, on the edge of laughter or tears. His facial expression was apelike: archaic, ambivalent. The old man said, Tell me, what brings you here. And the biologist was startled, forced to face that double glint again, that mouth so fleshy it almost seemed swollen, which this time opened to expose several teeth of different colors, some yellow, others almost purple, others white. I don't have all night, amigo, tell me, what brings you here, the old man repeated. The biologist's body shook the way cows shake at the slaughterhouse, sum of nervous automatisms, pure sacrificial body.

All right, if you won't tell me what brings you here, the old man went on, I'll tell you some things. Because hey, I like stories. I like them as much as the next guy. But

before I start, why don't you go and get one of those, he
said, gesturing to the jars of transparent liquid. The biologist didn't obey right away, but eventually he stood up,
went to the shelf, grabbed one, and sat back down. He
set the jar in his lap. That's right, son, hold on tight, don't
even think about breaking it, the man said, and licked his
full lips. Hold on tight, because that one's *your* jar. Yours
and no one else's, understand? That jar belongs to *you*.

The biologist dared for the first time to open his mouth.
Are you the Knight of Faith? he asked, straining to keep
his voice steady and not too shrill.

The old man's eyes creased; the plantation flames flared.
Me? he said, flattered. I wish, kid, I wish. No, amigo, I'm
just a worker, a technician, if you will. But if you want to
raise my rank, so to speak, go ahead. You can call me the
knight of formaldehyde. Here he let out an honest laugh,
and the biologist could see all the way to his throat and
the roof of his mouth, very red.

All right, all right, no more talking for you, said the
old man. Now it's my turn to talk. Now you keep your
mouth shut. From here on out, you've lost your tongue.
From here on out, you're as quiet as your jar. No turning back. And just think of all the trouble we could have
saved ourselves if you'd only talked when I asked you to.
What's so hard about talking to me . . . Anyway, listen,
I'll tell this one backwards and forwards. And hold that

jar tight, don't drop it now. Guard it with your life. Don't forget. Hold on to it, OK? Who knows what we might put inside. Something very precious, for instance. Something you can't live without. All right, first thing's first, let's get your story straightened out. You were living abroad for a while and had to come back, is that right? The biologist nodded. And since you couldn't find work, since you'd fallen flat on your face just like everyone else who comes back, you ended up at a high school, is that right?

The biologist had become a machine that nodded and couldn't stop.

Tough, the old man went on, that job was never right for someone like you, someone with all your experience, all your fancy degrees. Because you, sir, are a technician, just like me, a great technician. A guy like you has no reason to poke around in a dead zone like that, no sir, no way! But let's not get carried away. One step at a time. Let's get this all straightened out. You, sir, are a technician. A problem solver. So let's just say we're colleagues, the both of us like putting things in formaldehyde, so you, you and I are colleagues, we do basically the same thing, and both of us have to ask questions. That's normal in your line of work, and mine too—we both ask questions. But we don't ask them just for the hell of it, do we? No, we ask the *right* questions, we ask the questions that need asking. You don't open up nature's book like it's a direct line to God himself, no sir, you open it looking for something very specific. And I do the same thing, just like you but different, are we getting somewhere now? I open the book, I find whatever I'm looking for. Period. And then I shut the book.

The old man paused, got up from his chair, and located a brown folder from which he extracted some sheets that looked freshly printed. The biologist glanced sidelong at the text and saw that it was dense, illegible, no spaces between words, all of them made into jelly, and on top of that, set in ridiculous, infantile type—Comic Sans, maybe.

Let's see, the old man said, back in his chair and looking over the papers. We have the jar, and we have mister technician. Done. That's all done. What we're missing now is the story. It's a children's story. Listen, son, it's your lucky day: you get to hear the one about the machete. Who knows how many times I've told this story. I get a kick out of this one. It's no joke, OK? There's real juice to it. It's one of the old ones, the ones they've been telling for generations, way out in the middle of nowhere, are we getting somewhere now? That's all that really matters, that we understand each other, and that you hold tight to your jar. Don't you go breaking it, because then . . . It'd be a problem, let's leave it at that, so don't break it. In other words, hold on to it nice and tight. That jar is yours, just think of that jar as *you*. That's what really matters here, without the jar, there might as well be no story, there once was a man, an old campesino, rather, a viejito who lived with his granddaughter, because after a very long war, there was no one left in their family except the old man and his granddaughter, I mean, the grandfather and his grandkid, all alone in the world after the war. And guess what, their luck was so bad that the abuelito fell ill, he came down with something awful, so the two of them, grandkid and grandpa, went running to the village curandero, who lived way up on a mountain, far away from anybody else, as curanderos do. And this curandero had been an executioner during the war. He had to kill a lot of people. And with all that sacrifice, he also learned to heal. The man knew how to heal the sick. That's why he was the curandero, and that's why the old man and his little granddaughter went to see him, went running up the mountain through the night, up the tall, tall mountain, where the curandero lived, and they knocked on the door, desperate, of course, since the girl was still very young, a kid, really, and if the grandfather were to die, she'd be completely on her own. Truly alone. And the curandero got out of bed, and lit a candle, and went to open the door. And he took one look at the grandfather's face and knew exactly why they were there. He let them in, and he offered them aguapanela because it was

cold, and he said: Tell me, what brings you here, neigh-
bors. And they told him, oh, did they tell him. Look, the
granddaughter said, my grandfather's very sick, he's going
to die, please save him, I don't want to be an orphan. And
the curandero went and got some herbs from the basket
he kept them in, he mixed up some elixirs and gave them
to the old man, who right away got some color back. The
curandero said: Take this such and such times a week,
bathe this many times, et cetera, et cetera, and as he went
on explaining the treatment, they started to hear a sound.
Or more precisely: music. A voice that didn't belong
to a man or a woman, a very rich vibration, like metal
on metal. And all three of them—granddad, grandkid,
curandero—turned toward one wall, where that sweet,
sweet song was coming from, and the strangest part is, the
only thing on that wall was a very big and very rusty
machete. The curandero got nervous, his hands started
sweating. Forgive me, he said, I used that machete during the war. Who knows how many villagers I killed with
that machete. You know how it was. I had to. That's just
what I had to do. And even though these days I keep it
up there on the wall and only take it down to cut weeds
or clear the mountain every so often, the machete wakes
up and starts singing, especially if there's someone tasty
nearby. But don't worry. We just have to give it a little
drop of blood from the person who made it sing—in this

case, a drop of blood from your beautiful granddaughter. The grandfather agreed, grateful for the curandero's remedies. The girl was afraid, but she was so good she said nothing. The curandero took down the singing machete, and with the sharp edge of the blade, he cut the girl's arm very lightly, and yes, she cried a few brave little tears, but only a few, because really it wasn't much, just a nick. And the machete, the instant it soaked up that blood, it stopped singing. It went quiet. And the curandero put it up on the wall again. Are we getting somewhere now? The little girl stopped crying, the grandfather was cured, and they all lived happily ever after. Are we getting anywhere? Let's see. Let's straighten this out, piece by piece. You're the little girl, aren't you. Or are you the machete? I mean, come on, let's get to the bottom of this. You're out of a job. You're starving. You're a pitiful son of a bitch. Am I right? Poor bastard, no purpose, no pay, no bootstraps to pull yourself up with. That's it, kid, that's it, I see you're catching on. So. From what I understand, they offered you a job. Something new, something decent, fitting for a learned technician like you. Is that right?

The biologist was paralyzed, stiff in his seat. He was no longer able to speak.

OK, said the old man, tell me one thing: if you came back and fell on your face, if you had to eat shit in a shit job, if things were going so badly, why not take the job they offered you? That job might as well have been made for you. I don't see what the problem is. Or are you asking the wrong questions, are you opening up nature's book and looking for who knows what. You must be abusing our book. You must think you need to know. You're a little pretentious, aren't you? One of those guys who wants *wisdom*. A wise guy. Yes, that's it, we're getting somewhere now. What are you? I'll only ask once. What are you, son? A technician or a wise man?

The biologist didn't hesitate: a technician, he hurried to say in a thread of a voice, before returning to his garrote.

Then what's the problem here, said the old man, what is the problem. There's no problem here. Look, let's try something. This jar, which is yours and only yours, we'll keep this jar here, keep it empty. We won't put anything in it for now. Are we getting somewhere?

The biologist tried his best for a nod, yes, they really were getting somewhere.

But we'll hold on to the jar just in case, I'll take care of it for you. And you, you'll be reasonable, you'll get to work. Leave the jar on the table.

He did as the old man said, thinking for a moment he was saved, that the nightmare had come to an end. But the old man continued to stare, not saying a word, and a vast and frigid silence took shape between them as mighty clouds form around tiny flecks of dust.

Let me tell you a story, said the old man, and the biologist exhaled, already standing, his hand on the back of his chair. Have you heard the one about the machete? Sit down, son, sit down, the knight of formaldehyde said. Don't worry, your jar is safe. Have you heard the one about the machete? It's your lucky day, it really is. You get to hear the story about the machete. Listen close, now, it's starting. There's an old machete hanging on a wall. The machete senses the presence of a child, a beautiful child, and it sings. The executioner hears the machete's song and excuses himself to his visitors, the girl and her ailing grandfather, who've come for the executioner's expert opinion—the executioner's also the doctor. Forgive me, friends, forgive me, the executioner says, it's just that it's been a long time since this machete fulfilled its purpose, you understand. And sometimes it's overtaken by some kind of urge, and it starts to sing. But don't worry. All we need is a drop of blood from the girl. The executioner takes the machete down from the wall, and with its tip, he makes a small, a very small, cut in the little girl's arm. The drop of blood falls on the thirsty blade. The machete goes quiet. And then, in that shiny new silence, the silence of peace, the girl thinks: What a shame that song is over, the machete sings so well. What a nice sound.

Such an old sound. Metal music that crosses your body just as the stream crosses coffee fields or the forest. That's what the girl is thinking, but she doesn't dare say it out loud. Are we getting anywhere? the old man asks.

The biologist, incredulous, had partaken in the retelling of the story. He smiled now, stupid, permanently stunned.

You, sir, have no tongue, so you can't offer your opinion, the old man went on. But if you want, you can offer your opinion. Tell me your opinion. We put great store in your opinion, professor.

The biologist's mouth opened, mechanical, oval, and he inhaled a gust of warm air smelling of animal sweat. When the air came back out to the world, reheated inside of his body, it brought with it a few hollow words, eggshells of artificial intelligence: The beautiful child wanted to hear the song again, the biologist heard himself say, she was charmed by the song. She found the song charming.

That's right! the old man shouted. What else?

It was an ancient music, the biologist heard himself say, a music of metal forged in the furnace of sin.

That's it! Yes, sir!

And I'm the drop of blood.

Yes, professor! You're the drop of blood!

And I'm the silence that's there when the music stops!

The old man smiled and licked his feminine lips and showed his teeth, all of them different colors. Now you tell me the story, he said.

There was once a grandfather, said the biologist.

Good.

And a little girl who charmed him with her song.

Correct.

And a machete, lost in the forest and looking for its owner, the executioner.

That's it, professor.

And a drop of blood throbbing alone in the song's temples.

Are we getting somewhere now?

We're getting somewhere.

22.

They gave him his phone back and let him go at the end of a pasture of sleeping cows, right at the edge of a pine forest. The men told him to cross through those trees and go down the mountain, there was a bit of a path he could follow, and in an hour or so, he'd run right into the highway. Then, without saying good-bye, they turned and went back to the outbuilding, and the biologist stood there a few seconds, at a loss, in the light of the full moon. That's it? he thought, a little disappointed. They aren't going to kill me?

Euphoric, unable to contain his body's trembling, more and more perplexed, head crammed with dates and images, he jumped a barbed-wire fence and stepped into the forest. A dead forest, thought the biologist, the kind that's been robbed of its water, sucked dry. One more monocrop. Nothing could make it here. Just then he heard noises down by his feet, like a challenge to the thought. The noise of things dragging themselves, a collective sound.

In the light of his phone, he saw there were chickens everywhere, hundreds and hundreds of sleepless chickens, rooting around for food in dry pine needles.

The image left him so terrified that, even at risk of stumbling, he chose to turn the light off and walk as quickly as possible.

23.

That same week, he took the job on the palm-weevil project with his old girlfriend.

The biologist's life changed drastically in very little time. He started to make lots of money and focused, like the specialist he was, on the study of biochemical adaptations in the mating calls of one insect. He visited plantations to analyze in situ the behaviors, interspecies interactions, the environmental impact of the blight.

He also left his mother and moved into the house in the city center. He took pity on the old fuck and decided to let him stay, him and his wayward son. There was room enough for the three of them.

He adopted a stray dog and a pregnant cat that gave birth to six kittens, two of which survived.

The biologist was relieved to see things resolving themselves at long last. Everything was sliding into place.

Sometimes life improves if you just stop thinking so hard and devote yourself to your work. Two or three decisions are enough to right the whole. Better to stay as far from trouble as possible. Work grants us dignity. Clears the mind. I'm a technician. I open nature's book

to solve isolated problems. The work I'm doing has miti-
gated the palm-weevil blight, which was already starting
to take a toll on other virtuous crops, such as the peach
palm. The fruit of the peach palm is delicious. And to
think there was a shortage, they were selling them for an
arm and a leg at the market. Now the species is recover-
ing, thanks to us. What I'm doing is useful. There's no
reason to abuse the book of nature.

24.

Every Sunday morning, he went to the group home to visit his uncle. It was hard for them to communicate, but the biologist thought it was only right that he be there. Sometimes they watched TV, sometimes they read some book or sketched plants they recognized in the garden: thistles, lemongrass, mint.

Even as sick as he was, his uncle could draw much better than he could, so much so that the biologist hung up some sketches of his at the lab. His ex-girlfriend was always admiring them.

The patient showed no signs of improvement, but he also didn't seem to be getting worse. He's doing well with the medication, said the psychiatrist he'd been assigned, we'll just have to wait and see.

One of those Sunday mornings, they watched a TV show in which an evangelical pastor got up on stage with a baby whose face was covered in hair. This child, he said, is a miracle. The miracle of life and the miracle of God's will. Amen. God our savior, have mercy on us. You who live in me and in my word. Bless this child, who is Our Child and also a part of your Great Work, in which every one of us has our role and our purpose, our own divine mission.

That night, the biologist dreamed that something with hair was floating inside the jar, his formaldehyde jar. He had to hold the light of his phone up against it to realize that there was a bear claw inside the transparent liquid.

When he woke up on Monday morning, he'd already forgotten the dream.

25.

The dealer was showering in the dark, the pitch dark, in absolute silence, eyes open, trying to access his visions of phosphenes and sparks. He slowed his breathing, allowed his retinas to adjust. He waited. That night, though, he saw nothing. Just layers and layers of black, then dark-blue veils that pulsed from the walls of the gray cement box. The darkness went closing in on itself, and the dealer, in the absence of humble explosions and iridescent marine cartoons, thought he saw something like giant petals, black and wet, a sleeping flower—the flowers out back that his mother and sister tended religiously, which folded up in the night to protect themselves, which made anyone want to run fingers along the amassment of fresh lips. And those giant blue petals, almost black, edged nearer to the dealer's muddied body, and suddenly, he was enfolded in a cocoon. I'm ready, the dealer thought, let's go, chirretes, just try me, I'll show you what's what, fucking vermin. Although the truth is, he didn't know what he was ready for, much less why those words had come into his head or who his imagined enemy was.

He cut the water and, without turning on the light, dried off with a rough towel, freshly laundered, smelling of blue soap, then got out of the shower.

After dressing and running a comb through his thatchy hair in front of an old greenish mirror, the dealer rolled the slimmest joint and climbed up on top of the scaffolding crowning the two hunchbacked floors of his building. From there, he had a view of the whole neighborhood, a vast density of zinc roofs and fiber cement and little gardens where people had planted papaya, plantain, and mango.

The dealer thought about his friend, the biologist, whom he hadn't seen in weeks. What's going on with him? Is he buying from someone else? I'll find out. And if he is, if that fucker's playing me, I'm done. I mean, if I run into him, I won't even look him in the eye. Who does he think he is. Or maybe he's trying to quit? I should stop smoking so much. I'm high off my ass all the time. My mom and my sister tell me to pray, give myself over to God, but I'd rather make a deal like that with the devil a thousand times over. With the devil, at least you know what you're getting into. Inhaling the last of the joint, the dealer part laughed and part coughed. Sell my soul to the devil and use the money to go to the ocean for the first time. That's what I'll do. Swim in the ocean at night. That right there's the real scene.

26.

On the eve of Holy Week, the air in the dwarf city over-
heated, and the guayacans in the park flowered early,
urged on by hot gusts that seemed to belong more to summer. The air swelled with pride, slow and sinewed as over-
proofed dough, and at the pool hall, someone had gotten
up early to shoot solitary cannons amid grime and cigarette butts and the stench of last night's beer. The sound
of the pool balls striking each other was audible from the
street, and so were the a.m. voices on a battery-powered
radio. The small man selling gelatina de pata at one corner of the clock tower noticed that the volcano was in
clear view, free from the clouds that almost always concealed it, and was kind enough to share the observation
with one of his customers. At the summit, they observed
patches of dirty snow. Another customer saw a flying
saucer go into the crater. The fruit at the market rotted as
quickly as possible so they would toss it into the landfill,
where it'd be eaten by pigs and horses. The river water
wavered, remorseful, and sometimes tried to swirl backward, who knows where. The seeds of some trees fell to
the ground with a menacing *tac-troc-tac-troc* and dented

the cars parked in their shade. It smelled like premature summer, and soon someone shivered from inexplicable cold, which blew from the depths of an icy hell heretofore unknown to science. The new disposable buildings threw open their windows to allow in these ancient and modern forces: they were bladeless windmills, windmills that had a hundred blind eyes, oblong, half-empty watchtowers, barely habitable, and inside were unknown hands, kneading the first arepas of creation. A photosensitive mold on the kitchen wall insisted on recalling the old alchemy of photography. New landscapes spawned and died precociously around backhoes. The climate was delicious, catastrophic and perfect, and under the duress of a new narrative regime that demanded beginnings only, the spiders could no longer weave their webs. The tree bark made sugary poisons that attracted a yellow wasp. It came over from northeast Brazil the year before.

The biologist entered his brother's room and began to choose shirts, pants, and shoes. Standing in front of the mirror, he tried on each item. He set the ones that looked good on him apart from the ones that didn't. The ex-girlfriend had told him he had to stop dressing like a broke student, and the biologist, if only to keep his new workplace free of those kinds of remarks, believed that the quickest solution was to make use of his brother's dress clothes. After all, he thought, the habit makes the nun. And it's a waste to keep all this clothing here, it's just fattening up the moths.

The dwarf city exceeded its dwarfism all across the valley, far above the tectonic plates in whose cavities lay the vacated dens of Christianity, where all that remained were flowers of fossilized flesh and a series of heads that used to be flies. The amnesiac statues went to and fro, mimicking styles of locomotion they'd seen in parasitic plants. The biologist was pleased to confirm that the pants only needed hemming. Now his old girlfriend would have to stop making those comments. A lost man found a trail of feathers in the forest. Little by little, thought the biologist, this house will become a house again and stop being the family museum. I'm going to live in my house.

Go home. Go back to mammiferous love. Go back to original love. To original sin. Proactive enterpriser of counter-reformation, keep your chalice full and go back to the nest. Go back to the egg. Tend your own garden. Produce your own food. Go and live in the country. Make contact with forces of nature. Take my picture with your old camera. Take pictures of that landscape. Don't say that. We don't say that. Say whatever you want. Don't let anyone tell you what you can or can't say. Shut up. Love me the rest of your life. Bite your nails when we don't see you. Travel a lot, but come home. Go away to come back. Get by with whatever is there. Adjust. Adapt. Develop new limbs and amputate those that don't serve you, or let them atrophy, eat them for energy. Evolution is unavoidable. We're all changing. What matters is that we conserve. If you can't sustain, it's because you can't change. If you change, you sustain by changing. Reintegrate. Don't be conservative. Your leg isn't serving you? Ax it. Look: a falling star. Look: lightning in the field, and whinnying horses, terrified. How lovely it is to watch burn all we've so earnestly grown. Fight till the things you love are declared a world heritage site. Don't talk with your mouth full of dead animal. Don't be that way. Take off the mask. Be yourself. Show yourself just as you are. We want to see your imago. It's all zip-a-dee-doo-dah now. Help us. Your help could make the difference. We don't care what you do. Whatever you do, we'll understand. Quit with that tone. All extremists are the same. The ends meet. Extreme moderation. Find your natural place without moving house. Turn your trash into a source of affordable energy. Expect change. Everything's changing. You're changing. I'm changing. Don't fall behind. Get out early. Escape home again. There's no escape. My home is your home. The struggle goes on. As far back as Colombia's mountains. All of us changing so all can remain. Don't wait till they offer you work. Make your own work. Leave your work. Come with us, to the time of Restoration. Let's conserve water. Turn off the light, and look, the light's off. Now turn off the light. Sow softness. Sow song. Harvest good fortune and joy.

Translator's Note

"The detective novel must have a detective in it; and
a detective is not a detective unless he detects."
—S. S. Van Dine, "Twenty Rules for
Writing Detective Stories"

"No accident must ever help the detective,
nor must he ever have an unaccountable intuition
which proves to be right."
—Ronald Knox, "The Detective Story Decalogue"

Classic detective fiction starts with a crime and ends with
an answer. Truth is absolute, justice is assured, moral
codes are definite. Facts may be elusive, but they'll come
to light in time. All that's required is faith in the power
of reason.

Nearly a hundred years after its "golden age," the
genre has a well-established blueprint, its features and
formulas even preserved in lists—Van Dine's rules,
Knox's decalogue. The reader has clear expectations, and
the writer writes to fulfill them. Lucky for admirers of

Juan Cárdenas, those shared expectations make the form apt for subversion: if everyone knows the rules, everyone knows when they're being broken. "No more than one secret room or passage is allowable," writes Knox, in his third commandment. But in *The Devil of the Provinces,* Cárdenas takes the blueprint, cuts it to pieces, and collages it back together. The hallways are now secret passageways. The secret rooms are all hallways. There's no sense of inside or out. Are we building a building at all?

Hold this remade map up alongside the original and see a second narrative taking shape between them, about our own expectations of order and resolution, the limits and possibilities of perception, moral assumptions and attitudes. The genre's foundational works depict the world in schematic form to make it more easily solvable: "There must be but one culprit, no matter how many murders are committed." "No hitherto undiscovered poisons may be used, nor any appliance which will need a long scientific explanation at the end." "All supernatural or preternatural agencies are ruled out as a matter of course." Within this framework, good and bad are two unshifting poles; laws are just, and enforcers are justified; and crimes can be triggered only by individual evil, not circumstance, structural violence, or the coercions of economic and political systems. But *The Devil of the Provinces* works in the opposite way, bringing context to the fore to show how it makes accomplices of us all. Look again, Cárdenas urges: we're moving in a mesh of culpability. You tell yourself you're hero to the peach palm, but you're crisscrossed with big-ag and neoliberal capitalism. You wanted to get a job so you could leave your mother's spare bedroom, but now you're someone's political pawn, and you aren't even sure whose. No weapon can be ruled out, not when new poisons and long explanations and preternatural agencies are exploited all the time in the world churning outside the genre: Advancements in monocropping lay waste to ecosystems. Conspiracy theories brush aside climate change. A religious cult promising prophecy accrues wealth and political power.

The rules observed by Van Dine, Knox, and other early practitioners evidence a powerful guiding force in their writings, what scholars have described as a "radical rationality" that "affirms there are no threatening, unsolvable mysteries in the universe," only false theories that will one day be disproved.[1] You might say *The Devil of the Provinces* is guided instead by radical *irrationality:* there are no true theories here, or all of them are true. This novel, too, begins with a crime and a question:

---

1. Poeti, Alida. "Subversion and Reconstruction of the Detective Novel: A Reading of Leonardo Sciascia's *Todo Modo.*" *Italian Studies in Southern Africa* 11, no. 2 (1998). https://www.ajol.info/index.php/issa/article/view/112008/101768

a biologist's brother is murdered, and no one knows why;
the biologist turns sleuth, if mostly out of boredom and
inertia. But it ends with the understanding that asking is
futile, since the crime will never be solved. "Social order"
is shown to rest upon a foundation of state-sanctioned
violence and impunity. Deduction won't get you to cer-
tainty, let alone justice, and anyone who says otherwise
is sustaining the status quo. Every misdirection, com-
plication, and non sequitur breaks the false promise of
ratiocination, upending the hierarchy at the top of which
sit scientific rationalism, liberal individualism, and legal
justice.

As he reveals the ambiguities and contradictions that
sustain our social systems, Cárdenas alters the atmosphere's composition, cutting off access to the assumptions that made early works in the genre viable. The text
adapts to survive, like any animal—palm weevil or biologist. It's a horror story. A comedy. A fable with no moral.
It's a police novel in which police serve no purpose at all.
Refusing to adhere to the rules of any one style, or move
from conflict to resolution, or grant the reader the satisfaction of cause and effect, *The Devil of the Provinces* sug-
gests that we should be solving not just for a death, but
also for the places where our own lives intersect with it.

The tale of the machete at the thwarted denouement
enacts the same progression, like a miniature of the novel.

Contradictions abound. Sense is a matter of perspective. We peer through cycling linguistic and ethical lenses that distort as much as they reflect. "Tell me, what brings you here," says the old man who himself has sought out the biologist, who holds the biologist hostage. Then he tells and retells a story, each time reworking the system of signs that illuminate or obscure truth, each time drawing the listener deeper inside, until the listener, too, becomes part of it. "You're the little girl, aren't you? Or are you the machete?" "I'm the drop of blood," the biologist responds. "I'm the silence that's there when the music stops." The tension doesn't resolve, it ramifies, into another series of crimes and questions entirely.

Knox writes that "the criminal . . . must not be anyone whose thoughts the reader has been allowed to follow." Meanwhile, Cárdenas shuffles protagonist and reader through roles of innocence and guilt, investigator and culprit. Like the biologist who partakes in the story of the machete, we are first drawn into a shifting game and then asked to define it, only to realize too late that it can't be defined.

Lizzie Davis
Minneapolis, August 2022

Coffee House Press began as a small letterpress operation in 1972 and has grown into an internationally renowned nonprofit publisher of literary fiction, essay, poetry, and other work that doesn't fit neatly into genre categories.

Coffee House is both a publisher and an arts organization. Through our *Books in Action* program and publications, we've become interdisciplinary collaborators and incubators for new work and audience experiences. Our vision for the future is one where a publisher is a catalyst and connector.

LITERATURE
is not the same thing as
PUBLISHING

Funder Acknowledgments

Coffee House Press is an internationally renowned independent book publisher and arts nonprofit based in Minneapolis, MN; through its literary publications and *Books in Action* program, Coffee House acts as a catalyst and connector—between authors and readers, ideas and resources, creativity and community, inspiration and action.

Coffee House Press books are made possible through the generous support of grants and donations from corporations, state and federal grant programs, family foundations, and the many individuals who believe in the transformational power of literature. This activity is made possible by the voters of Minnesota through a Minnesota State Arts Board Operating Support grant, thanks to the legislative appropriation from the Arts and Cultural Heritage Fund. Coffee House also receives major operating support from the Amazon Literary Partnership, Jerome Foundation, Literary Arts Emergency Fund, McKnight Foundation, and the National Endowment for the Arts (NEA). To find out more about how NEA grants impact individuals and communities, visit www.arts.gov.

Coffee House Press receives additional support from Bookmobile; the Buckley Charitable Fund; Dorsey & Whitney LLP; the Gaea Foundation; the Matching Grant Program Fund of the Minneapolis Foundation; Mr. Pancks' Fund in memory of Graham Kimpton; the Schwab Charitable Fund; and the U.S. Bank Foundation.

The Publisher's Circle of Coffee House Press

Publisher's Circle members make significant contributions to Coffee House Press's annual giving campaign. Understanding that a strong financial base is necessary for the press to meet the challenges and opportunities that arise each year, this group plays a crucial part in the success of Coffee House's mission.

Recent Publisher's Circle members include many anonymous donors, Kathy Arnold, Patricia A. Beithon, Andrew Brantingham, Anitra Budd, Kelli & Dave Cloutier, Mary Ebert & Paul Stembler, Kamilah Foreman, Eva Galiber, Jocelyn Hale & Glenn Miller Charitable Fund of the Minneapolis Foundation, Roger Hale & Nor Hall, Randy Hartten & Ron Lotz, Carl & Heidi Horsch, Amy L. Hubbard & Geoffrey J. Kehoe Fund of the St. Paul & Minnesota Foundation, Kenneth & Susan Kahn, the Kenneth Koch Literary Estate, Cinda Kornblum, Sarah Lutman & Rob Rudolph, Carol & Aaron Mack, Mary & Malcolm McDermid, Daniel N. Smith III & Maureen Millea Smith, Robin Chemers Neustein, Alan Polsky, Robin Preble, Rebecca Rand, Paul Thissen, Grant Wood, and Margaret Wurtele.

For more information about the Publisher's Circle and other ways to support Coffee House Press books, authors, and activities, please visit www.coffeehousepress.org/pages/donate or contact us at info@coffeehousepress.org.

This translation received support from
Translation House Looren and Art Omi.

[loːrən]
Translation House Looren

Juan Cárdenas is a Colombian writer, art critic, and translator and author of seven works of fiction, including, most recently, *Elástico de sombra* and *Peregrino transparente.* He has translated the works of such writers as William Faulkner, Thomas Wolfe, Gordon Lish, David Ohle, J. M. Machado de Assis, and Eça de Queirós, and was named one of the thirty-nine best Latin American writers under the age of thirty-nine by the Hay Festival in Bogotá.

Lizzie Davis is a translator, a writer, and a senior editor at Coffee House Press. Her recent translations include Juan Cárdenas's *Ornamental* (a finalist for the 2021 PEN Translation Prize); Elena Medel's *The Wonders,* cotranslated with Thomas Bunstead; and work by Valeria Luiselli, Pilar Fraile Amador, and Daniela Tarazona.

The Devil of the Provinces was designed by
Bookmobile Design & Digital Publisher Services.
Text is set in Garamond Premier Pro.

9 781566 896771